Otherworld Origins ~ Book 2

Altered

Julie Scholfield

Silver Book Press

ISBN: 0-9983729-3-5
ISBN-13: 978-0-9983729-3-8

DEDICATION

To my husband Michael who helped me realize my dreams

CONTENTS

to fully Awakened." Rob blurts out.

"Fully Awakened? What does that mean? Why haven't you talked to me this way? It would have been helpful in the mine that is for sure." I reply.

"Well, you aren't fully Awakened yet." Rob says. "Not even close."

I look at Nickolai and he looks at me the confusion obvious on his face.

"How do you know I'm not?" I ask.

"Because I cannot speak to you mind to mind. I have a hard enough time just picking up your thoughts. Plus there is the whole change you never went through." Rob replies.

I thought that because I'm descended from two different Fae was the reason there wasn't much change?" I look over at Nickolai, who shrugs, and then look to Rob.

"We will discuss this more later. There will be plenty of time for you to get your questions answered and in detail by those that know more about your family. Right now, we need to get going." Rob turns to Bain, clasps his upper arm, nods once before turning and walking out of the enclosure of the trees.

It feels like I got dismissed. I don't like it. I look back at Nickolai for a moment, turn and run after Rob with Nickolai close behind me. I may not like what he just did, but I don't want to get left here either. I run pass the tree line and continue to where I think Rob went.

"Stop!" Rob's voice calls out. It's so loud it almost hurts my ears.

I stop abruptly and turn towards the sound of his voice. "Why were you hiding over there?" I ask Rob as Nickolai stops behind me.

"I was not hiding. If you go too much further, those trees will thin out. You will run straight off a cliff!" Rob walks closer to me and takes my hand. A look of concern and thoughtfulness crosses his face. "I thought you would be able to see where I went but I forgot that you cannot follow the trail that I leave yet."

"Trail?" I ask.

"Magical Trail. I know you will be able to see it once you are fully Awakened, if that is what you choose to do." Rob replies.

"Oh."

I didn't know what else to say. It seems there is more to being fully Awakened than he really wants to tell me. It almost feels as if he thinks I'd not want to should I know everything. It just makes me curious as to what the big secret is that could possibly change my mind.

"Come on, we have a ways to go, and without you being able to move as fast as Nickolai and myself, it is going to take at least a day to get to the palace." Rob motions for us to follow him as he slowly makes his way toward the direction of the trees.

The dense trees abruptly thin out and reveal a sharp drop

off. The sun is shining brightly and the blue sky is dusted with light wispy clouds. A large forest spreads out in full view below the cliff. The trees look huge and I can only see the tops! Large birds circle above a section of the forest and dive down sporadically into the canopy. I can hear something off in the distance but I'm not sure what it is. I look over at Nickolai to ask him what he thinks the noise might be and find him staring out towards the forest.

"Is that where we are going?" Nickolai asks Rob as he points at something in the distance that I can't see.

"That is it. It will take another day to reach." Rob replies.

"What do you see?" I ask Nickolai.

"A tall gleaming white spire. I assume it's tall since its poking up above the treetops." Nickolai answers.

I walk closer to the edge of the cliff and take a look down. A low cloud seems to be hovering below, obscuring the ground underneath it. I turn to ask Rob about what we will find down there when the ground beneath my left foot crumbles. I scream as I start to fall.

CHAPTER 2

Nickolai

Avalon's scream rips me from the fuzziness that has been clouding my mind since we reached the cliff. I see the look of terror on Avalon's face before her hair whips up in front of it and she plummets towards the ground below. I dive for the cliff edge in hopes to catch her. Avalon's fingers slip just out of reach of mine and I watch her fall in horror.

Out of the corner of my eye, I see something jump off the side of the cliff and dive down toward Avalon. It's Rob! His body straight and ridged, arms outstretched, he almost reminds me of Superman. I watch as he grabs onto Avalon and suddenly his iridescent wings pop out and lift them up in the air. With Avalon cradled in his arms, his wings start to move up and down.

The pair of them do not seem to be moving upward too fast, but the fearful look that was on her face has been replaced with what I can only imagine is a feeling of awe. His wings seem to struggle with the extra weight as he tries to lift both Avalon and himself back up to the top of the ledge. I reach down and grab a hold of Avalon as they draw near and pull her back up onto the ledge with me. Rob relieved of the extra weight, flies up landing softly next to Avalon.

Well I doubt he will be flying her down there. I smirk to myself. Rob is not as strong as he likes to think he is. I look over to the pair of them. Avalon is still a bit on edge but if we are going to get anywhere we need to start scaling down the cliff the hard way.

"Since you won't be able to fly her down there," I tell Rob. "I would suggest that you fly close by while we descend, just in case she decides to have another clumsy moment. I'll go down first, and she can follow, this way if she does fall again it can be controlled better."

Rob nods in agreement.

"Watch where I place my feet and hands, then swing yourself around the edge and try to follow me. I will catch you if you fall, and Rob will be there to assist too." I look at Avalon. She nods apprehensively.

I scoot over to the ledge and swing my feet over and try to find purchase on the rock face of the cliff. Finding a short ledge I start to lower myself so Avalon can see the ledge my left foot is on while my right searches again for a hold.

I look up to find Avalon's face inches from mine. All I want to do is scramble back up and kiss her, but I know she is not ready for that. Ever since the plane ride, a couple days ago, things have been strained between us. I don't know if it will get better. I hope with time it will. She is too busy watching my feet to pay attention to my face. I glance back down and lower myself further and I find a place to plant my foot. I start making grips with my hands into the rock face so that Avalon will have an easier time coming down. I grin at the new strength I possess that I didn't even know was possible before.

As soon as I'm a body length down I call out to Avalon to have her start her decent. I watch as she slips over the ledge. Her small feet reaching out and barely making the ledge before her hands have to find a new hold. Rob hovers near to keep her steady as she finds her grips. I can't help but stare at her butt as she moves to get better grip.

We descend into the low cloud cover nearer to the bottom of the cliff. The sounds I was hearing before seem dampened by the cloud, though, I think staring at Avalon's butt kept my mind where it needed to be. I chuckle to myself, a girl's butt keeping me from spacing out. Usually I space out looking at the butt!

"How much farther? My arms hurt and I don't know how much longer I can do this!" Avalon cries out.

"Give or take about 40 feet. If you are comfortable with it we can do a slow, controlled fall to the bottom from here." Rob offers.

Avalon sighs in relief. "That would be wonderful, thank you."

I watch as Rob takes Avalon from the rock face and manages to move them both out and behind me before slowly sinking downward toward the ground. Rob and Avalon come into view after another 20 feet. I toss my pack down to the ground before jumping off. I rotate myself to face out from the cliff face while falling to the ground below. I land with a loud thud, my feet stinging just a bit, but still manageable.

The sound I heard at the cliff's edge is louder now. My head almost feels like I've been drugged but I don't seem to care. The only thing I want is to find out where that beautiful sound is coming from. I start off at a jog, into the forest ahead.

"What the hell is that noise and where is he going?" I can hear Avalon ask Rob, but it is as if she is not important any more.

"Shit!" Rob swears.

I hear a scuffing sound and then both of them running after me. I speed up. I don't want them to stop me. I race forward, small low branches from the trees hit my body as I run pass but not caring. The trees clear and I find myself in a small meadow, full of tall grass and wild flowers. In the center of the meadow are three small, perfectly shaped women, dancing and singing in a circle. One has fiery red hair that seems to have a life of its own. Another has brown hair, that looks as rich as dark and milk chocolate swirled together. The last seems a bit taller than the other two with golden, wavy hair that trails down her back to her round bottom.

I stop abruptly, staring in awe at them. Something in the back of my mind, nags at me. Something I have forgotten, but the singing is so beautiful. I shake my head and start to move forward towards them.

One second I'm walking forward, the next I'm eating grass with someone on top of me shoving something into my ears.

"What the hell?" I call out. I turn over and push Rob off of me.

Rob mouths the word, 'music' and covers his ears. I realize I don't hear anything and my mind doesn't feel hazy. I look over at the women in the clearing, they have stopped dancing and singing. They are just standing there glaring at Rob. What a shame. It was fun to watch them dance. I grin, in spite of myself, remembering the way their bodies moved.

I remove an earplug and turn to ask Rob something, when the most beautiful voice fills the meadow.

"How dare you treat our guest in this manner!" The blond woman yells at Rob. "We wanted him to come dance, and join us in our merriment."

"It is how you go about your merriment that I do not condone, Alexia. First, you lure your 'guests' as you call them with fantasies with your undulating bodies and hypnotic music. Then you give them food and drink from our land so that they will never want to leave! Your 'guests' then become slaves to your amusement until you tire of them and then the rest of us have to clean up your mess." Rob counters.

"At least we can offer him a gift, not of food but of appreciation." Alexia says as she walks seductively towards me.

"No. Thank you for your offer of a gift though, Alexia, I am sure he appreciates it." Rob says sardonically as he steps in between Alexia and I.

Suddenly the woman's face contorts in rage, sharp pointed teeth bared menacingly. Her hair that was vibrant and beautiful, changes into short, blond, stringy unkempt hair. Alexia's face looks old and weathered, like someone who reached 100 years old and forgot to die. The body that was once enticing, is withered and bony. How could someone be so beautiful one minute and the next look like that?

I start to back away. Rob had mentioned not saying thank you for anything before we came to the Sidhe. So why did he say it?

"Your true form is so unbecoming Alexia, go back to your grove, no one wants your kind of gifts." Rob says with authority.

Alexia hisses as the other two women pull her back and lead her away towards the forest to the east. It makes me wonder exactly who Rob is here, how he has such authority over these people. I make a note to find out more later once we reach our destination.

CHAPTER 3

Avalon

Rob motions Nickolai to follow him. They walk towards me from where I watched everything from the edge of the meadow.

"Well that was, um, interesting." I say with a smirk on my face.

I'm having the hardest time keeping a straight face. I look over at Rob who has the smallest grin on his face. I look over at Nickolai whose face is an interesting shade of pink. I feel sorry for him but something between us has changed. I don't feel the same way towards him like before, and I'm not sure why.

I bend down and pick up Nickolai's bag. I hold it out for him as he reaches to take it. He doesn't even bother looking at me. Rob walks on past back towards the woods.

"We have a little farther to go. I believe no one wants to camp near those girls anytime soon." Rob says.

I turn around and look at Rob and I see him turn just slightly and wink. I know he is digging in at Nickolai and it is funny. I lower my head down quickly to hide the grin spreading across my face.

We continue on, deeper into the woods. As the sun begins to set, I wonder if we will ever make it to a camp for the night.

After what seems like forever, Rob announces, "We will camp here for the night."

He moves away from the large tree that he led us to and starts to gather small dry sticks. I hear a small noise off to my left and notice Nickolai is doing the same thing. I bend down and grab Nickolai's pack and bring it over to the large tree with me. All I can think about right now is my aching feet! I sit down at the base of the tree and rub my poor feet. I'm so not used to all this crap!

"Nickolai, can you finish gathering fire wood and make the fire, I'm going to go look for dinner for Avalon and myself?" Rob asks him. "Oh, and remember to ration what you have at the moment until we get to our destination. There should be more food for you there."

"Sure thing." Nickolai replies.

Rob walks over to the tree I'm sitting by and pulls out a bow and quiver that seems to come from inside the tree! He squats down next to me, I'm still rubbing my feet. He smirks.

"I'm going to go catch our dinner, I shouldn't be long. Are you going to be okay?"

I laugh softly.

"I'm fine, just not used to walking this much. I'm glad you know what you're doing, because I certainly don't know how to rough it quite like this."

Rob smiles at me and touches my shoulder for a second. He stands up and walks off into the woods.

I watch Nickolai for a moment as he is still gathering wood for the fire. A fire I know he really won't have much use for. So much has happened in the last 72 hours, sometimes I just want to pinch myself to see if I will wake up, hoping this has all been a bad dream. I know it isn't.

Finding out that I'm not only a supernatural freak, but heir to a throne in a place I didn't even know existed, was majorly overwhelming! Add to the fact that I'm not "Awakened" as Rob and Nickolai like to call it. Just what am I then? I had the "water" like Nickolai says I did. I ponder this for a moment. The crackling and popping of burning wood and movement I sense behind me brings me back to my surroundings.

Rob walks back into camp carrying three medium sized rabbits by the ears. He stops by the tree and stashes his bow and quiver back into the trunk. The fire is already steady and providing heat without letting off a lot of smoke, thanks to Nickolai. Rob sits down next to me and pulls out his knife. It looks like he is about to skin those dead rabbits right here. Gross!

"You aren't going to do that right here are you?" I look at Rob uneasily.

Rob chuckles softly.

"No, I guess not. I will be right back." Rob says as he grins back at me.

It's almost if he is having a small private joke at my expense. He picks up the rabbits and walks off to the other side of the camp.

Rob sets the rabbits down and goes to a nearby tree to cut down what looks like some small thin branches. I have no idea what those are for but I'm curious how he's going to prepare those rabbits. I just don't want to be that up-close and personal with the whole process. I continue to watch him work as he squats down next to the carcasses and begins skinning them. He then removes something from the bodies and places it inside the fur. I can guess what that is but I'm glad I can't see it. Rob grabs the thin branches and skewers the carcasses with them and sets them aside.

What is he doing?

Rob starts digging a hole.

Why is he digging a hole?

Rob then places the fur and the innards into the hole and begins to bury it. Then it dawns on me. Burnt fur might not smell too good so burying it must be the next best thing to keep any unwanted wild animals away.

Rob picks up the prepared rabbits and brings them back

over to the fire and hands a stick to me. I take the stick uneasily and clumsily put the rabbit over the fire. Surprisingly, there is not much blood on the meat. Rob sits down next to me and puts the other two over the fire to cook. I look over at Nickolai, who is looking glumly at his granola bar. It's got to be rough on him, I feel kind of bad that I can eat this and he can't. Before we entered the Sidhe, Rob warned Nickolai about eating or drinking anything found here. I'm sure he'd love to shift and go hunting on his own.

The smell of cooked rabbit brings me out of my thoughts. I carefully remove my dinner from the fire as Rob removes his at the same time. We sit in silence eating.

"So what is the plan for tomorrow?" Nickolai asks, breaking the silence.

I look over at Rob who wipes the juice from the meat away that has dribbled down his chin with his sleeve. He quickly swallows his bite before speaking.

"We have a good distance still to cover before we arrive at the Palace. If we leave early, we'll be there by mid-afternoon. Once we get to the Palace, just allow me to do the talking until all is settled." Rob states.

Nickolai nods. There are so many questions that I have about the palace and my family. I wonder if my brother will be there to greet me when I get there. Rob looks at me for a moment like he is waiting for me to voice my thoughts, then returns to eating his dinner.

"What do I do with the rest of this?" I ask Rob pointing at the remains of my dinner.

Rob looks over at me to see what I'm talking about.

"You will need to bury it." He replies. "On second thought, just leave it with me and I will bury it with mine when I finish."

I nod and put the remains near Rob before settling down next to the base of the tree. I lean back and rest my back and head against the trunk before closing my eyes.

"Do we need to set up a watch?" Nickolai asks.

"Yes. Thanks for reminding me. Go ahead and get some rest, I will take first shift." Rob says.

I hear Nickolai prepping for sleep, scooting his backpack on the ground and the movement that follows. I try to ignore both of the men. Anxiety has been building up and is still gnawing away at my mind making it hard to sleep. I worry how my family will receive me. Will they be happy to see me? Will I live up to their expectations? Will Rion be with them? If I am the girl of the prophesy, like Rob seems to think, shouldn't I have more confidence in myself? I worry that I'll let everyone down. I hear a low humming, a song that sounds so comforting and familiar at the same time but I can't seem to grasp where I have heard it before.

~*~

I follow Rob down what seems like a large hallway. There are people milling about but none look familiar. We reach two large doors that bear the Triquetra symbol, the same as on my necklace. Rob pushes the doors open and escorts me inside. The room quiets then suddenly plunges into darkness.

I have no idea where I am. I grope around for a hand, an arm, anything. I finally find Rob, glad he stayed close by. A small light flickers nearby, face is so close to mine, but it's not Rob. His warm, caramel and chocolate brown eyes have a silver ring around the pupil, marking him as non-human. The color and the warmth I see in them makes me want to melt into a puddle in the floor. The smile that is on his face is apparent in his eyes as he looks into mine.

He murmurs something that I can't quite make out, but the tone and quality of his voice makes me feel like home. I lean forward trying to catch what he is saying, the words seem a bit jumbled. A hand grasps my upper arm and pulls me back. The man disappears from view.

I hear faint sounds of a lullaby. I still don't recognize it. It is the only comforting thing in this sea of blackness.

Suddenly a loud voice booms out, breaking the comfort brought by the soft song.

"You will use your true voice when talking to me!"

I sit bolt upright, no one is around me but Rob looks over at me and arches a brow.

"Something wrong?" He asks.

"No. Just a good dream that I wasn't ready to wake up from." I lie.

It was partially true, but the voice I heard disturbs me.

"I hope I was in it." He grins.

"You were, but not like that." I snicker slightly.

I settle back down to try to sleep some more. I just hope I get to see more of the man with the yummy brown eyes again, or get to meet him soon if he is real.

CHAPTER 4

Rob

I am nudged awake by a large hand on my shoulder. I look up and see Nickolai walking back over to his pack near the fire that is still going strong. My eyes feel like they crusted over during the short time I was asleep. I rub them quickly along with my face. Time to check the traps and get the meat cooked for the rest of the day. I get up and stretch my limbs. I check Avalon who is still sleeping near the base of the tree. I walk off to check the traps I set yesterday.

After grabbing the five rabbits in the traps that I set I walk back to camp. I sit down by the fire as I need to get these cooking and ready to go quickly. I skin and remove the innards from the rabbits before skewering them on the sticks from last night and propping them over the fire. I throw insides into the fire to let them burn to ash. I go and cut down some more small branches and use the twine from the traps to make a small drying rack. I place the rack near the fire and put the skins on it so that they will dry out and harden a bit, making perfect carriers for the cooked meat.

The smell of cooked rabbit seems to rouse Avalon as she stretches slowly before sitting up. Her hair is a mess, but she is still beautiful. She catches me looking at her and I grin sheepishly. I know I'm caught, no point in trying to hide it. I remove the meat from the fire and put it in the skins, which are now dried a bit, tying them up with some cords. I stand up and wait for Avalon to be ready.

~*~

We leave the protection of the forest and quickly walk into a beautiful edge of an expansive sea. The fog surrounding the bay is so thick, it blocks out the sun and makes the day seem dreary. I lead the others to the waiting boat tied up to a small wooden dock. Better to take the boat then add another day to our trip. With these two, there is no telling what we would get into if we don't.

Nickolai is the first to enter the boat. His movements so sure and steady, he barely rocks the boat. He sets his pack down and sits at the bow of the boat. Avalon climbs in next. I swear that girl is the clumsiest Sidhe I have ever seen. I hope her Awakening will fix that but somehow I have my doubts. I don't look forward to her lessons that will be coming within the next day. I untie the boat from the dock and enter it, taking a seat at the stern.

"Rob? How is this boat going to move? There are no oars or motor?" Avalon asks turning back to look at me.

"Easily. You will move it through the water." I grin back

at her.

"We just go straight across and that is it?"

"That is all." I gesture for her to begin to move us forward.

Avalon turns back around and visibly relaxes. Nickolai looks at me in disbelief. I smile at him, knowing she can do this. The boat starts to move slightly then rocks back to where it was.

"I can't do this it's too hard." Avalon complains.

I lean forward and whisper in her ear. "You can do this and you will do this. You just need to believe in yourself Princess. I have seen you do what I would have thought was impossible. I know you can do this."

I sit back and grab onto the seat just in case she rockets us through the water. Nickolai notices my movement and grabs the sides of the boat.

Avalon lets out a puff of air and then quiets down. The boat starts to move slowly and picks up speed. She turns slightly and grins back at me with an impish gleam in her eye. Was that all just an act?

Judging the rate at which we are moving and the distance to the other side of the bay, we should arrive in about 30 minutes. The ride is surprisingly smooth. I sit back and enjoy the wind in my face and the salt in the air from the sea. The sounds of seagulls and other aquatic life fill the air. This a great start to what I hope will be a perfect day.

The boat rocks from being jarred by something. There are no large rocks on this side of the bay. I look over the side of the boat and I see them. Their dark shapes under the water surround the boat. I swear under my breath. Faces begin to pop up out of the water surrounding the boat, Merrows of all shapes and sizes are all looking at Avalon with curiosity.

"She commands the waters as if she is one of us, I can feel it!" A female adorned with jewels on her body calls out to the others.

"But what is she? She is certainly not one of us. What do you suggest we do, Aethelon?" A young male asks as he looks toward a larger male Merrow also adorned in jewels.

I had not thought the force of Avalon's power would call to them and beckon forth the leaders of the Merrow community. They were sketchy at the best of times, depending on their mood. We could have a fight on our hands or they could leave us be. I watch the two leaders as they look toward each other and hold each other's gazes for some time. The fact that I cannot listen in on their mind to mind conversation bothers me.

The female breaks the connection and swims towards the starboard side of the boat. Her mannerisms do not show that she means harm but is still curious as to who Avalon is.

"I am Maridine, Co-Ruler of the Merrows." The female Merrow states.

She looks over at Nickolai and dismisses his presence. She turns and looks at me, a look of recognition passes her face and her right eyebrow raises yet she says nothing before focusing on Avalon.

"My name is Avalon." Avalon says warily.

"I must know who or what you are. You have immense power over the water I can feel it, but you are not one of my people. Please, satisfy my curiosity, I just need a sample." Maridine asks.

"A sample?" Avalon asks then looks at me in worry.

"A small sample of your blood. I will not bite it will just be a small prick on your finger." Maridine explains.

Avalon nods and holds out her right hand to Maridine. Maridine holds her hand firmly before taking a pin hidden within the jewelry adorning her chest. She jabs the pin into Avalon's index finger quickly then puts the bloody end into her mouth. Maridine's eyes widen in shock before she quickly bows her head to Avalon.

"Please forgive me. I did not know." Maridine cringes.

Why would a ruler of the Merrows be acting like this toward Avalon? Can she tell by the blood her true heritage? I start to panic. If they know she is heir to the high throne this could mean trouble. Before I can say anything Avalon begins speaking to her.

"I'm not sure why I need to forgive you. What do you mean?" Avalon asks quietly, making sure only those of us in the boat and Maridine can hear her.

"You are of my family line, a direct descendant of my older brother. I can tell through your blood, but you are also

24

something else entirely. The power I have tasted within that small drop is quite overwhelming." Maridine whispers with fear in her voice.

"Then we are distant family." Avalon smiles down at Maridine. "As long as you do not wish to harm us, there is nothing to fear."

"I thank you, but you do not understand. You are the true ruler of our people. I have no right to command them any longer." Maridine bows humbly before Avalon again.

Avalon glances at me with an astonished look on her face.

"Then, I ask that you rule in my stead, until such time that I deem to take my rightful place." Avalon says firmly.

Wow! Spoken like a true ruler. I was afraid Avalon was going to need a lot of training in how to respond to situations like this. She rose to the occasion as if she was born to it.

Maridine turns and looks at Aethelon for a moment. He nods in acknowledgment and looks up to Avalon with a seductive smile on his face. I look at Avalon who seems to be completely oblivious. Maridine seems to have noticed and turns back towards Avalon. Her features change to almost a snake like appearance, scales erupting all over her upper body. Her green hair is now closer to whip like cords covered in scales. Her hands looked more like claws with long sharp talons. One look at Avalon, Maridine's face and body transforms back to the beautiful form of a mermaid.

The effect sends Avalon quickly moving back a bit shifting the weight in the boat slightly. A look of apology quickly forms on Maridine's face.

"I am sorry about that. I thought you may have for a second wished for my mate to be your own. I can see that you do not." Maridine explains. "You have every right to claim my life for my actions."

Avalon looks confused for a moment.

"That won't be necessary. You were reacting to protect what is yours. I would have done the same. I don't take offense." Avalon waves Maridine off.

Maridine nods and lets out a series of shrill calls. The Merrows all bow slightly toward the boat before diving back under the water.

I let out the breath that I did not realize I was holding and loosen my grip on the seat. The turn of events and the outcome was surprising but I am not about to look a gift horse in the mouth.

"Avalon let's get moving. We lucked out just then. However, we may not be so lucky if the Selkies find us." I urge Avalon to move us quickly.

CHAPTER 5

Melanie

I don't know what possessed me to think that I'd be able to handedly control 25 new vampires. Borderline crazy? It is certainly taking longer than I remember it taking me to get myself under control. I wonder why my experience was so different from what they are experiencing. Is it because I was surrounded by the stink that was Nickolai or something else?

I unlock the last cage and open it. The man in it slowly gets out, stretches and walks toward the others. I sigh in relief. So far so good. It has only taken few nights to get to this point. Finally, they can all just take a sip of blood from a bag without tearing into it. I don't trust them around general population yet, but there are so many of them I need to get them out of here and back to the house soon. The blood bags in the storage room are quickly depleting with all the failed attempts.

"We will be leaving shortly to go back to the safe house."

I call out to the group.

All 25 pairs of eyes stare back at me in excitement, no doubt ready to get out of these dingy caves.

"Since there are so many of you we can't travel the way you were used to before. Tonight you will learn how fast you really are. While we are moving you will follow me and will not stray from the path I take." I pause for a moment waiting for them all to acknowledge what I'm saying.

"You all know the smell of human blood and how sweet it smells. It's far more potent when warm and pumping through veins. If you smell it, hold your breath and keep running. I would hate to have to kill you because of your lack of self-control. Do I make myself clear?" I look at each individual directly as they nod in understanding.

I go into the store room and remove two backpacks from their hooks on the wall. I open up the cold storage units, I'm not even sure there is enough in here to fill both bags. I load up the bags, one full and one half. I double up the packs on my back. They may able to show control, but I don't trust any of them yet with this much blood. This supply should really last us a month or more if it is used as a supplement with animal blood.

I walk back to the room where I left the others, quickly counting 25 heads as I enter.

"Let's head out. Remember my warning." I call out before heading out of the room.

~*~

The clean mountain air is the first to greet me as I leave the mines with the others. I pull Nickolai's cell out of the pouch of one of the packs I'm carrying. I check it for cell service, as Estes Park is known to have some dead spots. I place a call.

"Speak to me." Drew's voice booms out from the phone.

It's the first time I have used a phone since my change. I pull the phone away from my head quickly, my ears ringing from how loudly he comes across.

"Drew, its Melanie." I say in response.

"How did things go? Wait, where is Nick and why do you have his phone?" Drew rapidly fires at me.

"Things went as well as could be expected, I guess." I pause for a moment.

"Carl didn't make it and Avalon was, well I don't really know what that was or how to explain it. Whatever she did, it was freaking awesome and frightening all at the same time. Water was everywhere!" I shudder at the thought of all the water, the people that probably drowned in the mines and down in Estes Park.

"Water? Holy shit! She's responsible for all of the flooding?" Drew asks in disbelief.

"Drew, how bad is it?"

"The Thompson River overflowed and washed out parts of Hwy 34 so you can't come back through there. It joined up with the Platte and the St. Vrain Rivers, flooding out parts of Greeley and Kersey just south of here. The house is fine, not in the flood path. Mel, where is Nick? It's been a week since you guys left!"

"Nick is gone. I found something interesting on my way back that has kept me just a little busy!" I snap back.

"You don't mean…"

Drew sounds as if he is choking up. I realize how it must have sound.

"No. Sorry I didn't mean it that way. He isn't dead. Due to Carl not making it, he went with Avalon and Rob. Apparently cell phones don't work where they went and he wanted me to contact you."

"So what was so interesting that has kept you away for so long?"

"Twenty five new vampires that I found locked in cages. All from work! It's been a nightmare trying to get them all under enough control to move them!"

"Move them? Here?" Drew asks incredulously.

"Where else would I move them?" I say in exasperation.

"You have a point. Are they ready to move now?"

"I hope so. We are headed your way tonight. We will be there before sunrise easily. I'm going to take them where we are least likely to run into people to avoid any accidents."

"Good idea. I'll start blocking out windows and the

sliding door down in the basement as a makeshift bunk room for them all until we can work on a better solution.

"Thanks. I have some blood bags with me that I will need to store somewhere when we arrive. I'm going to need your help on this. I have no freaking clue what I'm doing!" I confess.

"Understood chica. I'll see you soon!"

The line clicked off. Doesn't he know that you're supposed to say goodbye at the end of a call? I shrug and put the phone back in the pouch.

~*~

The air whipping around my limbs feels exhilarating as I run through the wild terrain of the Rockies. The group follows close around and behind me as we travel in a northeast direction trying to avoid populated areas. I take brief sniffs occasionally to make sure there are no humans nearby. It is rather curious that I can run this fast without really needing to breathe.

Out of the corner of my eye, I see one of the new ones fall back. Then another and another. I turn to look and see four or five make a beeline to the west. I scent the air and swear under my breath. Humans!

"Whatever you do. Hold your breath now and do not breathe until I say." I watch as those remaining nod in ascent. "Follow." I command the others as I take off running. I'm so angry right now I could tear something apart. I'm hoping that I don't actually have to.

The buildings of a small town come into view. There are not many buildings, but finding which ones were entered, before something happens, seems impossible. I stop the group on Devil's Gulch Road, in front of the Glen Haven General Store.

"We need to find them and fast. When you find them pull them away from the town as far as you can and hold them there. If any have killed in their thirst, I will deal with them." I call out.

The others nod and split up into five groups of four. Brittany stays with me, which means four, not five, are here somewhere. I just hope the others don't succumb to their hunger before we can get the four out. I sniff the air again to judge where the humans are and if there is a blood scent. The scent of humans is stronger out to the northeast of the store. I can feel my fangs start to drop in anticipation because of the scent but I ignore it. The last thing we need is to have a blood bath and alert Morcant that we are still alive and out here.

Brittany and I approach the first home. There are three people here. Their heart beats are slow and regular, suggesting that they are sleeping. I shake my head and move to the next home. I don't want to scent the air again unless I have to.

A scream cries out from the north. It catches me by surprise and I automatically scent the air. The sweet aroma of fresh warm blood fills my nose. My fangs fully extend, my mouth waters. I remember Maria and jar myself out of my blood lust. I slap Brittany to bring her out of her own blood lust. I look around and notice no lights have come on, maybe the other humans didn't hear?

I run toward the source of the scream with Brittany following close behind. The front door of the old brown two story home is still closed. A small window on the second floor is open, the white lace curtains softly flap through the opening. I crouch quickly and jump. I sail through the open window and almost land right on top of someone. I turn quickly and catch Brittany before she lands on them.

I turn around and lift the Vampire off his victim by the back of his neck and survey the damage. Her throat is mauled open. Blood is sprayed everywhere. It reminds me of Maria. I pass him off to Brittany.

"Hold him. I need to make this place look believable for an animal attack. Damn moron!"

My nails lengthen approximately five inches before I start tearing into her body. The body is still warm so it won't look like it was done post-mortem. I tear up the sheets on the bed and some of the furniture. I wreck the bedroom door and damage the stairwell all the way down to the first floor. I open the door and put several large claw marks on it. Then close it to put enough pressure on it to crack it in several places so the door will not stay closed. I grab some dirt and pine needles from the side of the house and trail it into the house and up the stairs. There is only a little bit of dirt and needles left when I make it back to the room. I rub them into the woman's feet to make it look like she had ran in from outside and was trying to get away from something. I survey my handiwork. Most will guess it was a mountain lion or a bear.

"Let's go. Hopefully this is the only one I have to deal with tonight." I motion to Brittany to follow me and we head downstairs.

Before leaving the house I look around. I remember what Nick told me about how to kill a vampire, that I needed iron. Near the fireplace is an old iron fireplace tool set. I walk over and grab the poker and it burns. It clatters to the floor after I drop it. The burn marks on my hand disappear almost instantly. To the left I see a towel on top of the counter in the kitchen. I walk over, pick it up, go back to the poker and wrap the handle with the towel. This will not be pretty when I have to use it, I look over the poker letting my imagination run wild, knowing what is to come. I walk back over to Brittany with the poker and we leave through the front door, with a walking corpse named Marcus.

~*~

The others gather around me back in the woods farther away from the town of Glen Haven. All four were recovered, only one will have to be dealt with tonight. It will be a lesson the others need to learn, and they will learn it.

"Does anyone happen to have a lighter on them? I know some of you used to smoke when we were human." I look around as the others dig in their pockets.

"Here." Matt calls out, tossing me his lighter.

"Thanks. I need a few of you to gather some wood, it needs to be dry so that it doesn't cause a lot of smoke. Once we are done here, we need to put the fire out quickly and scatter the evidence." I advise the rest.

The wood quickly piles up I grab some old leaves and twigs and start the fire and wait until it is at a good height. I grab Marcus and drag him into the center of the group near the fire and force him to his knees. Either he is submitting or I'm a lot stronger than I thought.

"Do you have anything to say for yourself? Do you even comprehend what is going to happen and why it has to be done?" I yell at him, angrier for making me do this than anything else.

"Who the hell let her be in charge? We are all hungry. Why is she dictating to us what must be done? She turned the same time as us!" Marcus addresses all those that are gathered around us.

"You all did. I could have left you to rot in that cage. You decided to join me. Your own stupidity and greed sealed your fate." I spat back.

Matt steps forward. "She has helped us all through this. The Melanie I remember before this happened, wouldn't have given a damn. No offense." He positions himself to the side and behind Marcus.

"None taken. I know how I used to treat people. That way of thinking doesn't help our situation. Working together will." I watch as the rest of the group nods in agreement.

Without another wasted breath I nod at Matt. He grips Marcus tight. I plunge the iron poker into Marcus's chest, the sound of punching through flesh and bone makes me cringe slightly. Blood spurts from the impact and exit wounds as the poker goes all the way through. I look at Marcus for a moment and notice he has gone completely ridged. I know he isn't dead. I don't know how I know, I just do.

My nails grow out three inches long on both hands, I grab onto the top of Marcus's head, driving my nails into his neck and start to twist. My nails feel like they are cutting through steel. It isn't easy but I can feel his flesh give way. There is an audible crack when his head comes off in my hands. I throw the head into the fire. I have not taught any of the others about growing out the nails and using them as weapons yet. They stare at me in awe and some try to do the same. Some are successful, some are not. I motion forward those that are able and they also take a piece off of Marcus and toss it into the fire.

I know I've earned the others respect. I know they will now follow my directions, because I have our best interests in mind. There is only four hours until sunrise, but I stand there watching the flames lick and burn through Marcus' flesh within the fire.

CHAPTER 6

Avalon

Just my luck. When I thought things couldn't get any more complicated. Let's just throw in that you are also the rightful ruler to fish! If I get wet like that will I look as hideous and scary as she did when she released her glamour? I want to have a major freak out right now but can't. I have company. I always have company. When am I going to get some privacy around here? I hope it is soon because I can't keep up this false exterior much longer.

I'm thrown forward as the boat smacks into the shore, right into Nickolai's lap! So embarrassing! I was so preoccupied with what just happened I wasn't paying attention to how close we were to shore.

"Sorry." I mumble, my face turning redder by the second, as I clumsily try to get off of him.

"No apologies needed, I certainly didn't mind." Nickolai

replies with a husky quality to his voice.

"I bet." Rob mutters under his breath.

This is so awkward traveling with two guys that both like me. Nickolai, I don't even know what we are, if we are anything, at the moment. Rob, he's awesome, my knight in shining armor. Neither of them are from my latest dream. Both guys treat me very well but something is off. Is it me, or is it because of the latest dream? Now isn't the time to be delving back into my thoughts. I shake my head and awkwardly climb out of the boat.

I stand up and look around. The fine sandy shore does not extend far before meeting up with jagged rocks, with more trees lining the rocks. Great, more forest. Rob, Nickolai and I walk up the beach towards the trees. When are we going to get there already?

Without warning, I suddenly feel dizzy and start to fall. Two sets of arms grab me on both sides. I look around disoriented. This looks nothing like the beach we were just at, just a bunch of large trees, grass and dirt. It's darker here as the canopy of the trees shade us from the sunlight.

"What the hell was that?" Nickolai asks in disbelief.

"I haven't actually experienced that before. It was almost like a gateway but not." Rob looks down at me in concern. I have no words for him. If I did this I have no idea how. I shrug.

"Whatever that was, it cut the distance in half, and we are almost there now." Rob informs us. "Are you able to walk now or are you still dizzy?"

"I'm okay I think." I reply.

We continue walking and soon the trees start to thin out a bit. Just above the canopy, not far off in the distance are two large white spires rising up out of the trees. I look over to Rob who nods and smiles. Finally. I'm relieved to almost be done, but incredibly nervous for what is soon to come.

Rob grabs my left arm and brings me to a stop. Nickolai stops behind me. I can hear him sniff the air. Who does that? Oh yeah, Were thing. It's going to take me some time to get used to all this weirdness. I can feel a shift in the air but I don't know what it is or what is causing it. I feel like I'm being watched by lots of eyes.

Five figures drop from the trees surrounding us. Each figure is covered in mottled brown and green colored leather. Each wielding weapons pointed at us. My heartbeat begins to quicken. I'm about to panic when Rob speaks.

"Stand down. I know most of you are new and you want to show that you can do the job but scaring them is not necessary or the best thing to do right now." Rob addresses the figures around us.

"Avalon and Rob, Welcome to Tir na n'Og." Rob gestures to the land before us. "This is our escort to the palace. Skye, I want you to watch over Avalon personally."

A dark haired woman steps up behind me and gets a little close for comfort. I look at her, her yellow-brown eyes shine bright with a silver ring near the pupil. Her hair partially but intricately braided to keep her hair out of her face. Her sharply pointed ears twitch and I look back at her face, she is looking back at me. Oops, guess I shouldn't stare so hard or at least not be so obvious. She steps back slightly when I don't back away from her.

We walk through the woods and slowly a path starts to raise up and changes from dirt to a light colored stone. Trees line the walkway on either side. A large archway comes into view, it is made of wood and stone. The stone portions appear to have a lattice pattern to it and the wood weaves into it as if it grew over time like that. The walkway splits off just in front of the arch, going off to each side of the arch way on a raised walkway. It looks perfect for guards to be on watch but I see no one there, but I can feel them. How is that? Something moves against my chest, I look down and bring my hand up to my chest, nothing is there. Strange.

We pass under the arch and the walkway slopes downward. The walkway soon levels out with the ground and splits off in various directions but we follow the walkway that continues onward. Soon a stone structure that looks like an Irish castle seems to materialize out of nowhere right in front of us. We reach two large wooden doors that seem familiar somehow. The doors are decorated various symbols made of silver and gold, the largest symbol is made of both metals and when closed make the symbol of a Trinity knot inside of a circle.

The doors open wide without anyone touching them. Rob motions me to enter first. I step across the threshold and into a beautifully decorated hallway. I can hear Rob, Nickolai and Skye follow behind me but I'm too engrossed in what

I'm seeing to pay them much attention. It feels like I have stepped into one of my childhood fantasies from so long ago.

The marble floored hallway is large almost white with grey patterns swirled into it. The walls are made of stone but are decorated with paintings and ornate tapestries that seem ancient. There are a few small doors that I notice lead off from this hallway as I continue walking. I stop walking for a moment. The place has gone eerily quiet. I look around and all eyes are on me. Some eyes are full of curiosity, others with aloofness, but no one moves.

Rob lightly touches my arm and motions to continue on with his eyes. I nod. I wonder why he is not leading the way. Maybe it is some sort of protocol he is following. The butterflies in my stomach are multiplying. I reach another set of large double doors and I pause and look back at Rob who just smiles and nods. I take a deep breath and another step forward and the doors open on their own again allowing me entrance into a grand room.

The people in this room appear to be more finely dressed than those in the hallway. The women's dresses are long, light and have an airy quality to them, as if they should be see through even though they aren't. The men wear tailored pants with long yet loose, flowing robes. The people here are not all the same race either, fairies, elves, dwarves and others I don't have names for. I stop for a moment at the next sight that has caught my attention. There is a stocky man with dark brown hair with his back to me, but he isn't who caught my attention but the unicorn standing next to him. A freaking unicorn! The man turns around and grins. I know that face as well as my own. I take off in a run. I'm sure it is not proper for a princess to run like this through everyone gathered here but I don't give a damn. Rion grabs me into his bear hug that I have missed for so long.

"I have missed you so much! You have to tell me what you have been up to! What has it been like here?" I rattle off.

Rion laughs. "Slow down. There is plenty of time for us to catch up, which we will do as soon as you're settled in. They are waiting for you, and from the look on Grandfather's face, he doesn't seem too pleased with your behavior." Rion grins as he rolls his eyes.

I snicker. "We will catch up later then. Time to get this over with." I give Rion another hug and turn in the direction he looked when he mentioned Grandfather. The man standing on the dais at the back of the room does not look like he could be anyone's grandfather let alone mine. His long red hair flows down his back, his blue green eyes are piercingly bright. I look for any type of warmth in them, but I see none. No sign that he is happy to see me either.

I notice movement behind Grandfather that makes me stop mid-stride and catches me slightly off balance. Una! How? Before I can make more of a fool out of myself and fall in front of everyone a hand takes mine and steadies me. I look up to thank the man that has helped me and gaze into beautiful chocolate brown eyes, the inner circle of them like burnished gold complete with silver ringed pupils. Those eyes! There is humor lighting up those eyes. I can feel my face turning red. The man chuckles lightly and places my hand in the crook of his arm and slowly leads me toward the dais and the pair standing on top it.

I take several glances at the man as we walk forward. His long brown hair with its many streaks of gold is tied back partially behind his ears, the rest flows down his back. I have never been attracted to someone with long hair but for him I would definitely make an exception. The man is hot! His height makes me feel tiny. I feel the hard muscle of his arm beneath the sleeve of the cerulean blue robe he wears and my mind drifts off to imagining what the rest of him might look like under the robe.

A throat clears bringing me out of my thoughts and focusing on the person in front of me. Grandfather. I look up at him and I see a sparkle of humor within his eyes, as if he knows what held my attention captive for so long. I feel my cheeks redden again and then realize I'm still holding onto the handsome stranger with the golden chocolate eyes. Turning to the stranger I slowly and reluctantly remove my hand from his arm.

"Your kindness in escorting and preventing me from being even more of a klutz is appreciated." I say and nod my head to him politely.

"It's killing you not to be able to say 'Thank You', isn't it?" He bends down and whispers in my ear.

I look sideways at him, wondering how he knows. I can see he is playing. I nod again and smile.

"Until we meet again little one." The man says bowing slightly and returning to the gathered throng.

I watch him go wishing I could join him.

"Well I can see someone has caught your attention. You will have time to pursue that later." A deep male voice says.

I turn and look at my Grandfather who almost looks like he is about to start laughing. Maybe my first impression of him was wrong. The long platinum haired beauty, that looks so much like Una, steps closer. She shakes her head at me as if knowing I'm about to ask how this is possible. Obviously something she doesn't want me to divulge here. Is it because she is not supposed to leave and her visiting me as a child was forbidden?

"Hello Avalon. It is good to have you home at last." The woman says.

"Tha…" I stop myself, smile and nod. Not saying "thank you" is hard when it is so ingrained.

"I am Finvarra, High King of the Sidhe, and this beauty is my Queen, Oonagh." Finvarra states.

I dip my head not only in respect but to hide the astonishment I know is showing on my face. The woman I used to spend time with as a child, Una, is my grandmother! She hasn't aged! I remember something Rob said in Colorado, about how time does not move here like it does there. How old are these people?

"You will be taken to your rooms now and will be attired properly as befitting your position. Once that is done then I will announce you as my heir. I refuse to do so as you look now. I just hope very few can associate the waif before me with the princess you must be." Finvarra nods in dismissal before turning and walking away.

CHAPTER 7

Braelomdrel

In the twenty years I have been a fosterling, of Oonagh, never has the court been buzzing as much as it is today. I am not sure what is going on. I have to admit it has me a little intrigued and worried all at the same time. Oonagh is the only one here that knows my mother. Though with the time spent here, she is not my only friend. Finvarra tolerates me but I don't think he knows who my mother is. If he did, I would have been thrown out of the nearest gateway. According to my mother, they rarely ever got along. I do not know the history between them and the past seems a touchy subject whenever it is brought up with Oonagh. My mother tends to keep her secrets to herself until she wishes me to know. I hope all the buzz today is not about me.

I finish writing down my latest thought and close my notebook, wrapping the leather cord around it. Even though everyone is bustling about, it is still peaceful here. The sun's rays filtering down through the canopy of the trees gives a soft lighting to the courtyard. Birds are singing and chirping while squirrels are leaping from branch to branch, seemingly unbothered by the bustling of the court. I sit back on the bench and stretch my long legs. Before I can get too comfortable, I hear the call, signaling me to hurry and get to the Great Hall.

~ * ~

I walk into the hall and spot Rion talking in an extremely animated way to Caliweth, a council representative to the Unicorns. Maybe I am being a bit paranoid. Rion is my friend, and the grandson of Oonagh and Finvarra. If all of this was about me, I do.not think he would be excited and happy about it.

Whatever is going on, I know a full report will need to be made on it to Mother later. I sigh. I enjoy learning how things are run here. I have noticed how things could be better, not just for the Sidhe but humans as well. I just do not understand why Mother is so insistent on all this secrecy. It feels like spying.

I head over toward the dais upon which the thrones sit near the stone. Before I reach my assigned position at the base of the dais, the hair on the back of my neck stands up. I feel a pull that forces me to turn around and face the double doors of the Great Hall. The doors open and a small slip of a girl stands in the doorway, wearing a rather ragged and frayed white dress. Her dark hair has red streaks running through it. It is wild and unkempt but it looks good on her, most cannot pull off that look. There is something about her that makes me think she isn't as frail as she appears.

She bolts in a dead run through the hall. No one ever does that here! I find it rather refreshing and entertaining with all the stuffiness that is the norm here at court. I watch as she almost knocks Rion over. She must be the sister he told me about. Funny they look nothing alike. Rion looks similar to Finvarra but with darker features. This girl, I do not see any resemblance to Finvarra or Oonagh. Maybe she looks more like her father's family.

I wrack my brain trying to remember if Rion ever told me her name. If he did, I cannot seem to remember. I look back over to them and see that she is walking towards me. Well not me exactly. I can feel Finvarra and Oonagh's presence to my right and behind me. The girl's eyes seem to be locked on Finvarra. I don't really think she has even noticed me.

The girl trips, on what I cannot tell. Maybe she is naturally clumsy? Clumsiness is not a normal trait of her people. I rush over and help her steady herself by holding onto her arm. She looks up at me. The initial look on her face is gratefulness, but a look of shock quickly replaces it. Her lovely, rose colored lips part slightly and no words come out of her mouth. Her reaction to me is confusing. This girl is an enigma to me. Have I met her before and completely forgotten? I am sure I would have remembered this pretty little unexpected package. Her green-brown eyes are locked on mine. There is a faint silver ring around her pupil. Why is it so faint? The power I feel in her is much stronger than the ring suggests. I definitely want to spend more time with this girl, she is intriguing.

~ * ~

The dark haired woman looks at me in disbelief from the scrying bowl on the table.

"She cannot possibly be that strong yet. In time, maybe but I highly doubt she is as strong as you are feeling my son." Mother says.

"I can only tell you what I felt from her. The fact that she seemed to recognize me was unsettling. Do you think she knows who I am?"

"I highly doubt she does. She probably just fell for your handsome face." Mother smiles at me warmly.

I smile. I wouldn't mind getting to know her better.

"That is a look I have yet to see on your face. Pursue her. I think you will be good for each other. She could be what the people have been waiting so long for. Keep your origins secret for now." Mother warns.

"I will."

Mother's image fades from the water and I am once again alone in my room. I move over to the bed and fall onto it. Things are about to get a lot more interesting. Avalon, I muse. Her face hovers above mine in my vision. What is it about her that is so compelling?

CHAPTER 8

Rob

Watching the small exchange between Avalon and Braelomdrel, brings up a bit of jealousy. I cannot deny it. She had the same look in her eyes when she first saw him that she did when she first saw me. Well, sort of. There was the whole idea that I am not her brother that she had to get over. I thought we were getting past that. I sigh.

I glance over at my parents who are looking quizzically at me. I can tell they want an introduction badly. I know they have already noticed my attentiveness toward Avalon, and that it goes beyond mere duty. I nod to them and shake my head. They nod understanding that I meant yes you will meet her, but now is not a good time.

I wait patiently while Avalon talks with her grandparents. My mind wanders slightly to other matters that need attending. Nickolai. I need to get Nickolai taken care of as well. I motion

Rion over. I know he will help me get this taken care of as quickly and discretely as possible. Nickolai needs to be trained, but more importantly, he needs to be out of the way.

"Rion, I need you to take Nickolai and get him set up in the barracks. Inform Senna as well." I motion for Nickolai to join us. I wonder how much he will see through this to my other motive.

"Nickolai, while you are here you will be in the barracks and will go through additional combat training. Your skills, while good for human military, are sub-par for our standards. Rion will take you to get settled in." I watch as Rion ushers Nickolai out of the room.

I turn to see Avalon heading my way. I know that look. I just hope it is not directed at me. Her almond eyes are narrowed and the look on her face seems like she wants to either blast someone or beat the crap out of them. Her jaw clenches and unclenches as she continues toward me.

"Why the hell was I presented like this?" Avalon hisses at me

"It could not be helped. I had orders to bring you here without delay once we entered the Sidhe. No one, with exception of a few who will keep it secret, will know who the "waif" was after you are presentable." I reply.

"What. An. Ass! I don't care if he is the high king, or my grandfather! A little kindness wouldn't hurt!" Avalon blurts out loudly as she walks pass me to the double doors.

I turn and follow her. This could get interesting. No one leaves Finvarra's presence like that. They always agree with whatever he says!

"Avalon, slow down. You do not even know where you are going!" I call to her after passing through the double doors of the Great Hall.

"As long as I'm out of there, I don't care!" She says forcefully through gritted teeth.

I catch up to her and lightly touch her arm. She slows down a bit.

"I suppose you know where I'm supposed to be?" She asks but does not look at me.

I can feel her anger radiating off of her in waves. What did Finvarra do to piss her off so much?

"I do. If you will come with me, I will be your escort to the suite. Then I can give you the itinerary that you'll need for the rest of the day." I reply softly.

"How do you know where my suite is?" She asks, this time looking at me.

I swallow the hard lump that seems to have miraculously formed in my throat. "I know because it belonged to your mother."

Her lips form a silent "O" then quickly close into a thin line as she nods quietly. I know from experience it is time to change the subject.

"The schedule is light. Your grandmother did not want to overwhelm you on your first day. I think she had a feeling you and your grandfather might clash. Tomorrow will begin your lessons in etiquette, governing, history, combat and working with masters of the abilities you have shown affinity for so far."

She turns and looks at me as if I just grew two heads and horns.

"As the Heir, you must learn these things. Being who you are, you cannot fail to learn them either."

"What happens if I fail?" Avalon asks in small voice.

I stop her and bring her into a small alcove out of the way from any passerby.

"Is that what you are worried about? Failing?"

She nods.

"Okay, I am going to lay this out here. I did not speak of what happened back at the mines because of your Dad, but you must hear what I witnessed. Back there, you lost control. It was almost as if something or someone else took over. It was raw and magnificent! Once you learn to control whatever that is, you will not fail. That is why you are going to be trained by masters. Get the thought of failure out of your head."

I pull her into a fierce hug and feel her relax slightly, for the first time in days. I brush her hair with my hand and hold her close, knowing she needs this. I just hope she will start to want me as much as I want her.

"Rob." Avalon sighs. "Can you take me to my room please?"

I sigh. I do not want to let her go. I release her from my hold. "Sure, come on, it is not too far but there is a few flights of stairs to climb." I take her hand briefly, squeezing it quickly, before letting it go.

As we approach the ornately carved wooden door of Avalon's suite. I am reminded of Trieva for a moment. Even though I have not been to this room in almost 50 years, it is very familiar.

"Amberley, we are here." I mindspeak to the woman who is waiting beyond the door in Avalon's suite. I open the door for Avalon and let her step in first.

"Princess!" Amberley exclaims as she comes gliding forward, all smiles. "It is so good to see you again!"

Avalon gapes, her eyes wide. The look on her face shows she may have just reached the limit on information over load.

CHAPTER 9

Avalon

The body accompanying the voice that is welcoming me, almost sends me into shock right there on the spot. A lithe figure with iridescent skin with hues of blue, green, pink and silver, glides gracefully to the doorway of my suite. The filmy gauze-like dress she wears suits her, yet on a normal person, would barely cover anything. I glance down to her feet and they are not on the floor but hovering above the gleaming hard wood! I glance back up and look for wings but there are none! What is she?

"Excuse me?" I look at the female in front of me.

"Oh dear!" The woman's skin colors begin to shift, the look on her face seems troubled.

I sigh. Another surprise. I look at the woman and then at Rob waiting for someone to start explaining.

"Avalon, this is Amberley. She was assigned to you at your birth, to watch over you and attend to your needs." Rob starts to explain and then stops when he sees the look on my face.

I can't help it. I have had a watcher my whole life and just get told about her now? Where was she when I was in need of her? Why wasn't she attending me and seeing to my needs before? I know I must look like I'm ready to explode. I close my eyes and inhale deeply. I know what happened was not her fault and looking at her, I doubt there is much she could have helped me with anyway. She doesn't look much older than me. How could a baby watch over another baby, it makes no sense? I open my eyes and turn my attention to Amberley.

"I know this is going to sound extremely rude but, what are you and why am I just being told about you now?" I ask her.

"Milady I am sorry for this, I truly am. Your mother made me keep my presence secret to everyone. Upon her death she had me come back to the Sidhe to prepare for your arrival. I am a Changeling and until your mother's death, I was always with you." Amberley looks at me.

"A Changeling? Are there many of you?" I question her.

"I can change into many living forms; plant, animals and humans." Amberley begins to explain.

"Like Nickolai?" I interrupt.

Amberley looks confused for a moment and looks to

Rob. A moment passes and Amberley chuckles.

"No, I am a different race. Weres only change from human form to one animal. As to your previous question, there are not that many of us any longer, less than twenty. Many of my people died when our land sank into the sea." Amberley responds as her skin colors shift again, her face briefly showing grief.

"I am sorry to bring up a painful subject for you." I sympathize.

Wait. Sank into the sea? She couldn't possibly be from there, could she? How old is this Changeling, and is she actually a female? Well that will be awkward if she really isn't and my attendant, especially if that means what I think it does.

"Um. I don't know how to ask this." I trail off.

Amberley must see the curiosity on my face and giggles.

"I am a Changeling. Yes, I can be male or female, but I identify with the female form. I always have. If there is anything else you would like to know I will gladly answer it, there is no need to be shy." She explains.

I thought the amount of surprises I have had lately were enough. Now, this? It's just too much! My head feels like it is about to explode. I just want to have a nice warm bath and sleep, is that too much to ask?

"There is a warm bath that has been drawn for you just past that door there, clothes are laid out for you to change into. If you need help with anything just ask and I will be there to assist you." Amberley says quietly as if sensing my distress.

I nod my head and walk to the door she pointed out and opened it. Expecting bright lights of a bathroom to assault me, I squint my eyes in anticipation. The room is well lit by candles and scented with lavender and vanilla. The bathroom has a light stone flooring and marble counter tops. The fixtures look like they are brushed nickel and a large soak tub sits in the middle of the large bathroom surrounded by more candles complete with flowers floating in the water.

I peel off the dirty white dress that is now in rags, leaving it a pile in the floor. I slowly sink myself into the tub and sigh as the warmth of the water envelopes me. I close my eyes in relief and feel the tension releasing from my limbs. This is the most soothing place I have been in for a while.

I try to let my mind clear and drift off but certain things keep nagging at me in my head. My grandfather looks so familiar to me, but I've never met him before that I'm aware of. My grandmother, can she move from place to place at whim? How many people in my life have I met that aren't people but Changelings? If Amberley has always been with me until my mother's death, how come I never knew her before?

I shake my head slightly. I need to relax and let my mind rest. I clear my thoughts. A small orb of light begins to develop in my mind. It grows from a small ball until it almost seems to consume my field of vision. The light starts to fade and in its place is a pair of chocolate and caramel brown eyes.

CHAPTER 10

Melanie

Wasting time with Marcus and his stupidity was annoying but completely necessary. Now the others know I mean what I say and that I will give out punishment to the stupid. I still don't know why I seem to be faster and stronger than the others. One day I will find out.

We have made pretty decent time coming out of the rookies and across the river. The others were able to hold it together when we passed north of Fort Collins and started southwest. I'm proud of their restraint and willingness to not put the group in more danger.

I feel the change in the air first, which brings me out of my thoughts. The night sky is starting to lighten. I look back. The others are starting to get sluggish. Crap!

"Now is not the time to slow down!" I call out to them. "We have a bit farther to go. Dig deep and push yourselves!

We need to be at the house before the sun crests the horizon!"

"Why can't we stop somewhere closer or take shelter in the trees?" A voice calls out.

"If you want to pass out, be burnt crispy and in a hell of a lot of pain when you're finally conscious, be my guest! Follow me if you want to make the shelter!" I snap back and pick up the pace.

I see the outline of Carl's house in the distance. I start pushing myself harder. I really want to see Drew again before passing out. My body already feels like it is starting to rebel. Every pump of my arms and legs seems more strained.

The sky is brightening as the sun's rays penetrate the dark of night. I know we are racing against the clock now. Drew opens the back door and beings yelling at us to run faster. I can make it inside before the sun crests but I'm not so sure of the others. I reach Drew and the protection of the house before looking back at the others.

Like a wave has hit them, one-by-one, they start nose diving. The speed of their bodies impacting the field makes it look like small bombs going off. I cringe as Brittany does a nose dive right into a cactus. I know it won't hurt Brittany but it still makes me hurt a little for her. Then I see Brian, with his mouth open, as he falls face first into a pile of cow shit. I can't help but laugh. My laugh is cut short as I feel the darkness coming. It's up to Drew to get us inside.

"Sorry." I manage to mumble and collapse onto the concrete patio at his feet.

~*~

My eyes pop open in a sudden panic and I sit up just as quickly. Exposed! Outside! It is all I think of for the first second before I notice my surroundings. My room, well the room Carl said I could use. I sigh in relief. I owe Drew big for this. I get up, open the door and peek out of the room. It's dark but I can see the forms of the other twenty four still knocked out cold on the floor of the large basement.

They won't be up any time soon. For the entire time I've been around them, they always slept longer. What is so different about me than them? I close my door and rummage through the dresser. There are some really cute things in here! I pause for a second. No one had time to get more clothes for me when I was here last. Avalon was taken before she could come back with more. Everything happened so fast there really wasn't time.

Ew! The thought makes my skin crawl. I have been in the same clothes for a month! I groan knowing what this means. Now I really owe Drew big time. I grab some clothes and head to the bathroom. Time to start the day and pay up!

~*~

I head up the stairs after a nice shower and finally wearing clean clothes for a change. I almost feel like the old me again. Oof! I bump into a solid wall of chest and then arms come around me holding me tight.

I breathe in, it's Drew. My nose crinkles up. "Oh gag the smell!" I tease him my voice muffled in his shirt.

"Oh, hold your breath and shut up for a minute." Drew quips back.

I snicker and hug him back.

"You had me worried and scared you weren't ever coming back. I had no idea if you were even still alive." He pulled me back away from him and looked down at my face.

"Oh they would have to be much tougher than what I saw there to take me down. Well except for the totally creepy, hot guy." I grin back up at him.

Drew crinkles up his nose in disgust. "You think Morcant is hot?"

"Yeah he's hot, but his creepy vibe would make any sane girl back the hell up." I reply with a smirk.

Drew grins. "That's my girl."

"Only if you are lucky." I grin back at him.

"I could be lucky now right?" Drew waggles his brows.

I crack up.

"Well now that they are all here," Drew gestures to the basement. "What exactly did you have in mind? They won't like crashing in the basement together for very long."

"I was thinking that Avalon is going to need all the help she can get when the time comes, and that we," I gesture to myself and the basement, "can help her and get our revenge."

"After your revenge, then what?" Drew asks. The look on

his face doesn't seem completely focused on the ones down stairs but just on me.

"I don't know. I didn't think that far." I mutter.

"Well I don't have unlimited funds to keep this place going. Carl didn't give me access to his accounts. We can't afford, nor do we have the room to house everyone, Mel." Drew sighs.

"What if we pooled our resources? All of us. Then when its dark start working on an addition to the house. Attached to the basement and keep it underground. That way not only will we be able to add more room for the ones here, but we can keep them out of the sun and from attracting unwanted attention." I look at Drew for a response.

"That isn't a bad idea. As long as everyone else is willing to do that. We will need to wait until the others are awake before we can move forward with this." Drew says.

"We are up." A voice says from the staircase.

"I assume the 'everyone' you two are talking about includes the rest of us." Bryan gestures to himself and the others on the stairs.

"Come on up please. Let's gather in the living room to discuss our short term futures and where to go from here." I gesture to my left and let the group file into the room. The group sits and stands around the room waiting. I move to the front and for a moment, wonder if this is how Rob felt last month.

"With what has happened, we have all been placed in a

precarious position. This house is far enough away from town that we can live somewhat freely. The fields and wooded areas will provide ample hunting grounds. There is however, two problems. The first of which is room for everyone, the second is money to pay for utilities and other necessities like clothes." I tell them.

"Why can't we just go home?" Brittany asked.

"You have all been reported missing by your families or friends." Drew interjects. "If you were to return to your homes, especially those of you who are married, do you trust yourselves in your current state with your loved ones? Would you risk their lives just so you can go back home?"

The group shakes their heads in unison.

"What about those that live on our own, with no family or roommates?" Stephanie asks.

"It would be safe for you to get things that you would like from your homes or apartments if you would like. The problem would be your control. Do you trust yourself with your neighbors? Can you not bring attention to yourself?" I ask her.

Stephanie shakes her head.

"If we were all reported missing how do we get jobs to sustain income? How do we access our current funds especially for those that are married?" Bryan asks.

"I may have a solution for that. Young single people tend to move and quit their jobs on a whim some times. You will still have access to your accounts, you can still use your documents to find jobs but you will need to find jobs with graveyard shifts. For those that are married, get with me later and I will get you hooked up. Right now, in your condition, you are better off missing or dead than with your families." Drew adds.

"I believe you said there was a problem with space? I haven't had a chance to look around this place yet but if there is building and carpentry work that needs to be done, I have some experience in that." Justin chimes in.

"Oh, thank God." I breathe out in relief. "This house's bedrooms consist mainly on the main and upper floors, there is one room downstairs that I have been using since I got here. I'm sure that bunking together for a bit is annoying but doable, but it's not a viable option for the long term. I'm sure we would all appreciate our own spaces until we figure out what to do after Morcant and his followers are dealt with."

I watch as all the heads in the room nod in agreement.

"Justin, do you have any ideas on how to solve this situation? Is there a way we can expand underground with an entrance from the basement? If we can, I think it may be an ideal situation for a while so that we can stay together without being in each other's faces all the time. It will also not raise suspicion of our exact numbers in this house."

"Sure there is a way, it will be the supplies that may be tough to get with funds being low. With what I have seen we have an issue with iron is that correct?" Justin asks.

"Yes, iron burns but through the heart, it paralyzes us." I inform the group.

Justin glances out the window and notices one of the outbuildings on the property. "What is in that building there?" Justin points out.

Drew looks out the window at the building Justin is pointing to. "It's a shed with tools. It should have the items we need to do what you are thinking of doing."

"Alright. First we will need trees. Tonight we will collect trees from the wooded areas around here but not from this general area. Before you leave tonight make sure the tree you bring back can fit into the building, if it can't, cut it in half. We will make support beams and start our main tunnel tonight." Justin says matter-of-factly.

CHAPTER 11

Nickolai

The day has been a whirlwind. It is hard to know which way is up. First, the Merrows in the bay. I have never seen them go as ugly as Maridine did. I guess I've never saw their true form before. The shift we did from the bay to almost the front doors of the palace took the breath right out of me. I don't know how that happened, but from the look I saw from Rob at Avalon, I'm guessing she inadvertently did it. The brief stint in the Palace before being escorted out felt like I walked into a fairy tale. The natural architecture made of wood and stone, the well-lit corridors full of glowing orbs that float over our heads and the doors opening on their own with no door handles. It all makes this place seem like it is teaming with magic.

The barracks, those are a different story. I feel like I have been plunged into the Middle Ages! Well, not quite the Middle Ages, but the place has definitely seen better days.

The wooden floors are solid but worn. The walls are made of wooden planks and allow a nice breeze through the space. The roof is well made and the rafters makes me feel like I'm back at church camp when I was a kid.

"I see you were not able to come with much. That is not uncommon. Clothes will be provided and placed on your shelf every day. There is a new set here for you to change into." Rion points at the shelf inset into the wall next to the bunk I have been offered.

"Do you know where I can shower? It's been a couple days and I'm sure I don't smell all that pleasant." I say.

"I wouldn't bother showering right now. You will smell even worse soon enough." Rion laughs.

I look at him in confusion.

"Your training begins as soon as you change. They are waiting for you at the training grounds now." Rion replies.

"I take it you have already gone through this training?"

"Yep. It is no cake walk. They may go easy on you since it is your first day but the longer you are hear the harder it will get." Rion warns.

"I don't really have much choice. I owe it to your sister being here, and you too I suppose." I brace myself against what may come.

"I know what happened. I don't blame you for this. I don't think Avalon really blames you for it either. My dad went out the way he wanted, fighting to protect his family.

That you want to help will be enough." Rion says solemnly.

I nod.

~*~

I step out of the barracks onto a dirt path lined with trees. It is fall back home, the leaves were already starting to change colors when we left. The leaves here are a lush green almost as if we were in midsummer. The clothes I changed into almost reminded me of fatigues from the army in the way they fit and were a grayish green. I follow the path until it opens up into a field with three figures standing off to the side.

I walk slow and steady toward the three, cautious but confident. The group consisted of an Elven woman, a man, and a Dwarf. I blink in surprise. He did not look like the little people I had seen back home. His long blond hair was tied back with leather cord. His blond beard is gathered into a braid and reaches his waist. He leans on a small walking stick but for some reason, I don't think he really needs it.

"Never seen a Dwarf before boy? A gravelly voice questions me.

"I'm sorry for my rudeness. I have seen little people before but none have looked like you." I apologize.

"Little people and Dwarves are not the same. Do not be insulting. Little people are small statured humans. They are not Dwarves!" The Dwarf bellows.

"I'm sorry."

"Wow, not even gone ten minutes and you have already gotten on the bad side of Julz. Well to be honest that is the only side he has." Rion looks at Julz, a smile playing on his face.

"Watch yourself boy, your training is not over." Julz retorts.

I allow myself a soft chuckle.

The Elven woman steps forward and sizes me up.

"I am Senna. I will be your instructor. We will work on hand-to-hand combat, a variety of weapons and also your form. From the smell of you, I would guess some form of cat." She states quickly.

I nod and look to the man. If she was my instructor then who is he. The man grins. Right, these people can hear my thoughts.

The man chuckles and steps forward. "I am Zephyr, but some of my more stubborn friends call me Trigger." He looks over at Senna who rolls her eyes at him and smiles. "My presence here is to heal you when you need it and to provide training with a bow."

"Who says I will need healing? I heal pretty quickly on my own." I retort.

Zephyr chuckles again. "Oh I am sure you will need it now, especially with Senna and Julz if he decides to join in."

Do they really think so little of me, that I can't defend myself? Do they think I can't hold my own on the battlefield?

"You are used to fighting Humans right?" Senna asks.

"Yes, but..." I start to say but Senna cuts me off.

"We are not Humans. We are faster and stronger than anything you have been up against before. When you can best us, you will have no trouble with any of Morcant's goons." She says.

"I have had sparring sessions with Rob." I blurt out.

Senna chuckles. "I can tell you now that he was going easy on you. He is the best of us and he would not have sent you here if he thought you didn't need training. He assessed you during your sparring session. I bet he found your skills good enough for the task at hand but found you lacking in some area. Are you ready to test my theory?"

I nod. Julz, Rion and Zephyr back up to the edge of the clearing.

Pain! My entire body slams down into the ground. What the hell? Senna leans over me and looks down at me.

"Get up. It isn't time to nap!" She snaps.

I have no idea how she did that. I didn't even see her move! I get back up. My body is slammed back down to the ground, my head hitting the hard earth soundly.

"Will you let me get up already?" I say in exasperation.

"Let you? No, you need to get up and stay up. Stop me from putting you down, kitty cat." She teases me.

I let out a frustrated growl. I sense around me as I start to get up. I thrust out my arm and hit her hard, square in the center of her chest and she stumbles back slightly winded. She grins and nods.

"You need to use your senses all of the time. Use the power of your other form and its heightened senses. You will need them. Sight, sound and smell. Later, we will work on pulling up certain characteristics from your other form to use as weapons without fully changing. Do you understand?" She looks at me seriously.

I think back to when I saw Melanie doing something like this. Willing her nails to grow into deadly, sharp claws and then retracting them. I nod.

"Good."

I hear a noise to the right and notice Julz placing various weapons on a rack. This is going to get interesting. Who uses swords when you can bring a gun and end it quicker?

"You can use a sword to deflect the bullets if you are good enough." Senna says matter-of-factly as she glares at me.

I have to get used to my thoughts not being private. I grimace. I watch as she pulls a sword from the rack and looks past me. I turn and see Rion standing there with a small pail of water at his feet. I move out of the way, this is clearly a demonstration.

I watch as Rion brings up a multitude of small round globes of water. They take shape of small bullets and harden into ice. I guess Senna is about to prove her point. The bullets shoot out from Rion like he actually has fired a gun. I watch as Senna blocks each one. It's almost hard to see as she is moving so fast. I let out a low whistle. The barrage of ice bullets on metal stops. Senna gestures to the rack.

"Your turn." She states. "Pick your poison."

"You have got to be kidding! I'm not skilled enough to block that!" I yell out while walking toward the rack.

Senna and the others laugh hard. My jaw clenches and unclenches. I'm getting really tired of all this belittling crap.

"I am going to test your skills with your first weapon of choice." Senna chuckles lightly. "You will not be able to defend yourself like that with a weapon for quite some time." She adds.

I look at the weapons on the rack. I choose the two dark, solid daggers. I hear a grunt. I look over and Julz seems to nod in approval at my choice.

I walk back to the open circle where Senna waits for me, daggers grasped tightly.

I turn towards her, only to see her charging at me. I try to deflect the blow that is coming. I hear the sound of metal clashing with metal. I sigh in relief. Then my left arm starts to burn.

"Tsk, Tsk." Senna says.

I look at my arm and it is sliced open almost to the bone. What the hell? I blocked her, how did this happen?

"You were great on blocking the upswing, but you

completely missed the backswing." Senna says smugly.

Zephyr comes over and slaps some muddy gunk on my upper arm, mumbles something I can't quite make out and walks back. My arm no longer hurts. Was that English? I test out my arm. It moves like it was never injured.

"Again!"

I hear her light footfalls rushing toward me. I meet her blade with my own and quickly block the second swing with my other blade.

"Have you always been a quick learner?" She asks, almost in a pout.

"I usually don't repeat a stupid mistake." I retort.

She smiles. "There is hope for you then."

CHAPTER 12

Rob

"You have got to be freaking kidding me!"

I hear Avalon's voice through the door of her bedroom as I let myself into her sitting room. I chuckle to myself. I had wondered what she would think of our fashions. I definitely had my answer. I sit down in one of the cream colored chairs and wait for her to get done. I glance at the time piece on the wall. We still have a bit until the council meeting starts.

A few more moments pass and the door to her bedroom opens. I feel my jaw involuntarily drop slightly and I close it quickly. My stomach feels as though it has jumped into my throat. I fear saying anything. I clear my throat and adjust my cravat. The long dress coat I am wearing suddenly seems unbearably warm.

Avalon enters the room, her long dark hair is in a half up-do with her red highlights accentuating the curls. The cream

74

and green off the shoulder dress, hugs all the curves that count and flows lightly to the floor in a graceful train. I can only imagine her exclamation from before was due to the undergarments she must be wearing. She is stunning!

"Done gaping at me now?" Avalon asks with a smirk on her face.

"Not really." I grin. I'm caught and I know it, no use denying it. She laughs lightly.

"So why am I being dressed up so nicely?" Avalon questions me.

"You are to be presented to the council and formally announced as Heir. Oh, this is normal dress for you. The only exception would be for combat or ability training. You will need to get used to it." I reply.

"Used to it." Avalon states, with her eyebrow raised. "I know what will change when I start my rule."

I chuckle. That won't be the only thing to change here. When the time comes, it will be interesting times for sure.

"First, before you go to the council you need to learn to walk correctly in that dress. You also need to learn how to present yourself to the public."

"What is wrong with how I walk?"

"You have a tendency of looking down when you walk. You will trip over your dress doing that. A princess always walks with her head held high."

Avalon starts walking towards me, keeping her head up.

"Not so high than you will drown if it rains!" I crack up laughing and she giggles.

"Your chin should be parallel with the floor. You may have to do the old "book on head" practice later."

"You mean that is a real thing?" Avalon asks with wide eyes.

"It is a real thing." Amberley interjects. "Don't worry your Highness, she will be ready come the next council meeting.

I inwardly wince. I never told Avalon much on my titles except for being her guard.

"Highness?" Avalon looks at me quizzically.

"His Highness is the Prince of the Seeley Court." Amberley states matter-of-factly.

I bow gracefully before Avalon. "I am still lower than you, Princess."

"Who is the King and Queen of the Seeley Court?" Avalon asks, then looks at me. "Why haven't I met them?"

"The King and Queen of the Seeley Court are Oberon and Titania. You will meet them at the council." I inform her.

At the mention of the names of my parents, I could see Avalon's mind working. Their names are probably not unfamiliar to her. Knowing Trieva, she probably made up fantastic stories about people in the Sidhe to tell Avalon and Rion when they were young. If she used my old alias in her stories, it will not take Avalon long to guess my true identity.

I wait for her to say something else but she does not and returns to practice walking around her room.

"When presented to the council, you do not curtsy to them. You may nod your head slightly in recognition of them, but never curtsy to them. The only persons you need to curtsy to is your grandparents. Even Rion will bow to you." I advise.

Avalon bursts out laughing. "Oh I'm sure that went over well when he was told that."

"He has been here longer. He was taught protocol and behavior some time ago. I do not think he minds. He does not seem eager for the throne."

"The next thing you will need to learn is the curtsy. The curtsy is not the easiest to perform, especially for one that is not used to doing it. Watch Amberley and then perform it yourself. You will need to do it when you approach the High King and Queen in the Council Chambers."

I watch as Amberley shows Avalon how to perform a curtsy. Avalon tries it. She is so graceful one would think she had been taught at a young age. It was like second nature. I notice her head is bowed slightly.

"You need not bow your head to your grandparents if you do not wish to. The act of the curtsy will do." I advise. There is a glint in her eyes as she looks at me.

~*~

Avalon and I stand in front of the Council Chambers for a moment before I pat her hand that rests on my arm.

"I have to enter now. Please wait here, you will be announced to everyone shortly." I smile reassuringly at her.

Avalon nods. I can see the nervousness in her eyes and how she is starting to bite her bottom lip a little.

"Oh, one more thing." I whisper, tucking my fingers underneath the chain of her necklace, gently pulling the pendant out that was tucked in her cleavage. "Proudly display this now. You are the irrefutable Heir of the High Throne. You have nothing to worry about in there."

Her face grows red and the hallway seems to grow warm. I clear my throat and smile warmly at her before entering the room before us.

I walk down the aisle and sit down on the right side of the main aisle next to my mother. As heir to the throne of the Seeley Court, this was my place. I would rather be positioned behind Avalon after she arrives. I know she is safe here and no one would dare attack her, but I feel better when she is near.

"Is she ready?"

I look up and lock my gaze with Oonagh. *"In more ways than one I think. I hope the Sidhe is ready for her."* I grin slightly and Oonagh nods back. I can see the subtle look of worry in her eyes.

Black and purple smoke suddenly fills the other side of the room. Great, just what we need. She is rarely ever here.

"Mab, why are you here?" Oberon stands up and looks in disdain at the center of the smoke. The smoke dissipates and

Mab, in all her dark glory stands with her consort, before us. Her dark luxurious hair is half piled up on the top of her head, the rest in loose waves down to her small waist. She is slightly taller than Avalon. Her dark dress that looks made up of iridescent black scales hug every curve, accentuating her breasts and hips.

"I would not miss seeing the new heir for myself! I am entitled to be here just as you are. You pompous windbag. It is my right as the Queen of the UnSeelie Court!" Mab states with an authoritative voice. Her dark eyes gleaming.

"We are here to discuss your son!" Finvarra states eyes locked on Mab.

"I am well aware of that. He is the other reason that I am here." Mab states and looks at Finvarra like she wants to say something more, but sits down at her place within the council to the left of the main aisle. I wonder what she is wanting to say, but before I can wonder too much the bells chime.

"Announcing Her Supreme Highness, Princess Avalon, Heir to the High Throne." One of the guards in the back of the chamber calls out loudly before the doors to the room open.

Avalon steps forward, her head held high. She definitely looks the part of the Heir now. Her skin seems to have an ethereal glow to it, just like Oonagh's. As she reaches where I am, I wink to her and she smiles just a bit more. She performs a graceful curtsy to her grandparents, as custom demands, her head still held high. I look down for a moment hiding my grin. Finvarra notices her slight at not bowing her head to him but comes down the steps, as custom also demands. He offers her a hand and guides Avalon back up the stairs to the seat on the right side of his.

I look over to Mab. Her dark eyes focused on Avalon. The look in them not one of malice but one that seems to be impressed with what she has seen so far. Most would not have shown the audacity that Avalon dared to the High King.

A bell tolls and Braelomdrel approaches the front of the room to address the Council.

"From the reports gathered from various scouts and from his Highness. " Braelomdrel nods to me. "Morcant has been busy over the past few years. It seems as though he is starting to amass an army. He seems obsessed on feeding on Fae as well."

An audible, collective gasp comes from the room. Even Mab is in shock.

"Not just any Fae it seems, but Fae of at least two different lineages." Braelomdrel continues.

"That is rare. Most pairings like that do not work!" A voice yelled from the back of the room.

"From his Highness' report, Morcant has the Cauldron of Dagda. He is using it on Humans that have a recessive gene of a Fae. He is using the water to bring their Fae gene to the forefront. Some of these humans have been found to have more than one or a combination of Fae and Were. Such as the case of Avalon and Rion's father, Carl." Braelomdrel informs the Council.

I hear a few gasps. I look to Avalon, and Rion stands

behind her to her right side. The look on both of their faces is a sight to behold and I am proud of them. It is as if they are daring the council to say a word about their Were heritage. They both know of the prejudices against Weres.

"The royal Heirs are of all four of Earth's lineages?" A voice to the left calls out in disbelief.

"My grandchildren are of all four lineages. The rarest and best hope for our future." Oonagh states proudly yet firmly.

"What does Morcant gain by feeding on Fae?" A scared voice calls out.

"From reports gathered, power. He looks for the rare ones and feeds on them. We almost lost Avalon. Thanks to the bravery of his Highness, Nickolai a Were who is currently training in our barracks and the sacrifice of Carl, she was safely rescued before we lost her." Braelomdrel answers.

"What of the Prophesy?" My mother's voice calls out. "If Avalon is who we think, why would she need saving?"

I stand up. "Avalon has not gone through the Awakening. The protections of her identity placed on her by the council upon her birth have not been removed. She is only just learning what she can do. Yet, I have experienced her power up close. It is truly a sight to behold. She still needs to learn control and go through her Awakening Ceremony."

"Then we will leave her training to you and it must start with all haste. Even without the Awakening Ceremony. If her powers are as you say, she needs to learn control." Finvarra states with authority.

Finvarra turns to Avalon. "You have a decision to make, as all Fae within the Sidhe make once they become of age. It is your choice whether or not to go through the Awakening Ceremony, it is not one we force upon you. Oonagh will discuss with you the choices you have and the consequences of each choice. If you are indeed the Daughter of the Prophesy my dear, you are our best hope."

"Has Morcant or any of his people found the ways into the Sidhe yet?" Finvarra looks to me and then to Braelomdrel.

"Not yet your Majesty." We say in unison.

"Very well. All that are willing to fight against Morcant shall report to Lady Senna. I will not leave the future of the Sidhe in the hands of a possibility. We will defend our own!" Finvarra calls out to the room.

I feel the surge of energy through myself and the room. Soon everyone is rallying with Finvarra, calling for the arming of the Sidhe.

CHAPTER 13

Braelomdrel

I exit the assembly and walk to my suite. I cannot believe what I have just learned. Not only does Rob and some of the others think that Avalon is the Daughter of the Prophesy, she is also of all four Earthly lines! No wonder I felt she was different from any other. I would have never have guessed this however.

I pour water in the basin on the table and start to rinse my face. I blot my face dry with the towel that was beside the basin.

"It is about time you were done ruining the connection." My mother's voice fills the room.

I jump back startled. "Shit! Do not do that!" I look down at my mother in annoyance, to which she just laughs.

"Why are you so jumpy anyway?"

"Morcant is starting to raise an army. The Prince believes

he is amassing this arming against the Sidhe." I start to explain.

"Rion believes this? How would he know?" My mother asks in confusion.

"No, the Seelie Prince, Rob." I clarify.

My mother laughs slightly. "Interesting name he has chosen to go by this time. What has been decided?" She asks.

"Everyone seems to be rallying with Finvarra to prepare arming the Sidhe against Morcant." I answer.

"What about the girl?" My mother fires back.

"A lot of questions I had about her were answered today. It was quite enlightening." I start.

"Spit it out boy!" My mother's voice grows impatient.

"Well apparently she has exhibited quite the extraordinary amount of power for one not yet Awakened. The Prince and others believe she is that Daughter of the Prophesy. What is more, Avalon and Rion are also of all four earthly lineages!"

"Stick to plan. I have yet to see that boy lie about anything important. If he saw immense power from her already, I believe it." My mother commands.

I nod as her image in the basin disappears.

I glance outside. I have about an hour before the celebration feast and bonfire for our princess. I pull out a nice button-down blue shirt and some dark acid wash jeans. I want her to feel comfortable around me. Besides, I like the human clothes. I walk toward the shower, looking forward to the evening and my hopes for the night.

CHAPTER 14

Avalon

Four? I'm totally confused. Where is the forth coming from? My head feels like it is spinning. I don't know what my grandfather did in there, but I felt like a foul oil was sliding across my skin. Everyone that seemed so scared did a 180 degree flip and are now ready to go to battle? How in the hell does that happen so fast?

Rob escorts me back to my suite to change. There is a feast and celebration in my honor in an hour. Thanks to all that is holy, I don't have to wear this dress or corset for much longer. I just hope the next thing I have to wear is more comfortable than this. I mean I look gorgeous in this, but I want my jeans and t-shirts back.

"I will be by to escort you to the celebration in an hour. I know it has been a trying day for you. Tonight have some fun. Tomorrow will be here before you know it. Oh, your grandmother has requested a meeting with you in the morning." Rob informs me.

I open the door to my suite.

"You did very well today by the way. I am proud of you." He says.

"You sound like my dad saying it that way." I tease him. "Thank you. I will be waiting for you in an hour."

He turns a bit red. I doubt he wanted to sound like my dad, but I'm not sure how I feel about Rob. I need to keep it light. Rob nods in response.

~*~

Not quite the style I'm used to but I can work with this. The dark skinny jeans and green open shoulder top fits nicely. The calf high brown boots set off the look perfectly. My hair is finally unpinned and loose. I have to admit, I'm loving the curls Amberley put in.

I'm really looking forward to this party. Amberley told me it's mostly a party that the young will come to. The older ones will be there too but it is mostly for food and stories. She said there will be music and dancing too! I want to leave the room and go now but Rob should be here any minute and I already know Amberley won't let me leave without my escort.

A knock sounds at the door to my suite and I stand up to go answer it. The look I get from Amberley makes me stop where I am. She walks to the door and opens it, allowing Rob to enter to collect me for the party.

He looks great. His green flannel shirt brightens his eyes.

The sleeves are pushed up to his elbows. The shirt is fitted just right for him. It shows off his broad shoulders and tapers down to a slim waist, bunching slightly at the top of his stone-washed jeans. His tan hiking boots look like they have never been used.

"Ready?" Rob asks me.

"You don't have to ask me twice. Let's get the party started!" I say while jogging over to him with laughter in my voice.

He leads me out of my room with his right hand at the small of my back. I accept it as culture, even though I'm not used to it and walk with him out into the hallway. He takes my left hand and wraps my arm about his. The then holds my hand on his arm with left hand and we continue down the hallway. We head out into a large garden complete with stone benches and large fountains. Some of the plants growing here I never knew existed! It is almost as if some plants from the moon of Pandora, from the movie Avatar, are real.

We leave the garden and come to a large clearing that is surrounded on all sides by trees and shrubbery. In the center of the clearing is a large bonfire. There are several large spits roasting meat on the left side of the clearing. Tables are scattered around the outer edge of the clearing, some are occupied while others still stand empty. Light globes hover above, providing ambiance to the party atmosphere. Close to the bonfire there are musicians playing instruments and people dancing nearby. People are mingling and seem happy. A much different atmosphere than what there was in the Council Chambers for sure.

My eyes go wide and I pull on Rob's arm. "Don't tell me Legolas is over there playing some funny guitar!"

Rob howls with laughter. "I was not expecting a Lord of the Rings reference when it came to Zephyr. I should have with you. That is a Lute, not a guitar." He answers still laughing.

"Who?" I ask. I swear, the guy looks just like Orlando Bloom as Legolas in Lord of the Rings.

"Zephyr. He is our resident Healer and fancies himself a musician. He is quite good." Rob explains.

"So what is he? I notice you have your wings hidden again. Is he like you?" I question him.

"No, he isn't. He is of the Tuatha De, like you. His father is Dian Cecht, one of the original that came with the Dagda and your grandparents to Ireland before making their home here. He is around the Sidhe somewhere. The older ones tend to go off on their own a lot." Rob answers.

"I have to go speak with someone for a moment." Rob says as he unwinds my arm from his as we draw nearer to the musicians. "Can I bring you back something to drink?"

I nod. The music changes up as he leaves. The melody is not like anything I have ever heard before and I close my eyes to listen more intently.

"No matter the situation or what you are wearing; you always seem to be amazingly beautiful." A deep, rich voice says behind me.

I turn to look at who is talking, somewhat startled and flattered all at the same time. It's him! The guy from the Great Hall. I can feel the warmth rise in my cheeks.

"I am sorry, my manners, forgive me. My name is Braelomdrel." He bows before me a hand tucked behind his back.

"Brae... lem...droll?" I ask. I know I have completely butchered his name.

The man laughs. "Brae will do just fine." He smiles down at me.

"It is nice to meet you Brae. Officially." I smile back.

He moves his hand from behind him and offers a small delicate cream colored rose with red edges. I take it and smile back at him.

"Thank you, it is very pretty." I say and sniff the small bloom. Its fragrance is intoxicating.

"May I have the next dance?" He asks softly.

"I don't know these dances. If there was a slow dance of some sort that would be preferable." I reply.

"How about you watch the dance happening now with me, so that you can learn. The next slow dance is mine. Then we can join in with the others in a group dance. Trust me, no one here will laugh at you. You will have my full support besides." Braelomdrel says with a smile and a wink.

I smile. I can't help it. There is something about him that is hard to resist. "How can I possibly say no?" I ask teasingly.

"You can't." He grins back

I laugh. Braelomdrel leads me behind the musicians and together we watch the dancers. Some are adults and some are just children learning. The dance seems easy enough. Braelomdrel leans down and whispers into Zephyr's ear. Zephyr nods and continues on with the song.

I turn to ask him what he said. I open my mouth to speak with the song changes to one with a slower tempo, my question answered. Braelomdrel sweeps me into his arms into a slow dance right behind the musicians.

"This is the best excuse I could find to get you all to myself. I want to know all about you." Braelomdrel says.

I blush slightly. "I figured my life was an open book here. What is it you don't know? It seems as if most people here know more about my life than I do."

"Oh. Well I know the basics, but that doesn't tell me about you. No one knows what you can do, that has been kept secret. I can feel the power within you and it is a bit terrifying but exciting all at the same time." Braelomdrel explains.

"Are you afraid I will harm the Sidhe by being here?" I ask quickly.

"No. Not exactly. I know most of the Sidhe, but I worry for Oonagh, my foster mother." He says.

"My grandmother has nothing to worry about. When I was younger, she would come to see me during my nature walks in the park. She was my best friend. I always looked forward to the time we would spend together. Then for reasons unknown she stopped coming, I never understood why. Whenever I told my parents about her, they pretended she was an imaginary friend."

Braelomdrel looks at me in shock.

"Why are you looking at me like that?"

"Your parents kept you in the dark your whole life? They never told you?"

"They tried to. I always knew there was something different about me. I could do things others couldn't." I explain.

"What things? How did you do it anyway?" He still looks confused.

"Do what exactly?" Now I'm confused.

"Visit the Sidhe without a Gatekeeper?" He says.

"I have never been here before. My grandmother always came to see me." I reply.

Braelomdrel shakes his head. "That is not in her power to do. She cannot move between the veil like that."

My mind starts whirling. If my grandmother couldn't come to me, that means I had to have done it. How did I go to the Sidhe when I had never been there before? How could I manage to be at the same place each time and my grandmother was almost always there?

"You look distressed. Are you okay? I am sorry if your

distress is any of my doing." Braelomdrel says softly, his face inches away from mine. The concern on his face seems genuine.

"I will be okay. I just have more questions. It seems to be a common theme in my life lately." I mumble.

"I am sure all of your questions will be answered shortly. You have only been here a day after all." Braelomdrel takes my hand and loops it into his arm. We start to walk back to the dancing circle. "I hope you don't mind if I call upon you again. I would very much like to know you better. May I see you again tomorrow?" He asks softly.

"I would like that." I smile. "You are the first person I have had a conversation with that doesn't seem to be hiding something. It's refreshing."

Braelomdrel smiles back, leans down and places a soft kiss on my cheek. I feel the heat raise in my cheeks as I smile.

A throat clears. I look up and see Rob standing in front of me, the look on his face is unreadable. He holds two cups in his hands; one drained completely, the other still full. Mine.

CHAPTER 15

Melanie

I can't believe how fast everyone has worked on the housing project. The tunnels under the house are no longer dirt and wood beams. There are actual walls and cement flooring. Several small bedrooms have also been made so that everyone can have their own little space if they want it. I keep waiting for squabbles to break out between the Vampires but maybe it is because they have a singular goal that they have not had time for much else.

Drew has been more than patient and actually kind to the Vampires I brought home. Home. It seems odd to call Carl's house my home. It truly does feel like home though. Normally, I would wonder why he doesn't bring any of his kind here as well. The current housing situation would not accommodate them, and I doubt the Weres would want to live underground if more rooms were made. Still it must be lonely for him.

The fake identification Drew was able to obtain for some of us has been extremely helpful. One of the girls obtained a job at a local blood bank. Easy bag swipe once a week has helped balance our diets and kept the supplies up. The bags I brought from the mountains will only last so long. With this many Vampires in one place wild animals will start to get scarce. We will have to keep running out farther for food.

A knock on my door brings me out of my thoughts. I put my pen down and close my notebook.

"Come in."

The door opens slowly and Drew pops his head through the opening. "Hey beautiful," Drew says. "Want to go on a hunt with me? It's almost dusk."

I smile broadly at him. "I thought you'd never ask." I grab my sneakers from the floor, near the foot of the bed and put them on quickly.

I haven't had much alone time with Drew since I came back with the others. Lately I have been wanting some alone time with Drew, to figure out these feelings I have and if he really feels the same or if he is just flirting with me. I need to know if the feelings that I have are real or just there because I'm feeling lonely. Wouldn't it be better if I tried liking one of my own? Easier maybe, not necessarily better.

"Ready to go get stinky with me?" Drew jokes as I join him at my door.

I laugh. "You're the only one that gets stinkier hunting." I grin at him.

"It's called manliness." Drew shoots back.

"No. It's wolfiness." I quip and head toward the stairs, Drew chuckling behind me.

~*~

Running through the brush towards the Rockies with the wind on my face and whipping through my hair, it feels so good. Even though it's fleeting, the feeling of freedom is long overdue.

I have no idea where Drew is leading me but he asked me to follow him. All I know is that we are somewhere northwest of Fort Collins and approaching the foothills rapidly. With Drew shifting right after we left the house, I didn't get a chance to ask him where. Following a Werewolf is horrible. Moving around with dog smell constantly in my nose any time I sniff the air. Yuck. I continue on out of curiosity.

I take another tentative sniff bracing myself for Drew's dog scent to assail my nose, but instead of just him, there is another animal. It has to be close. I abruptly turn right, running up the rocky hillside, not caring about following Drew any longer. I take another whiff and the smell of the animal in the air blasts my senses and my fangs elongate. I scan the rocky outcropping and spot a young buck making its way through the snow and large rocks.

Before the wind can shift alerting the buck to my presence, I strike. I take down the buck in a rolling tumble my teeth stuck firmly in its neck, draining the animal as we fall to the ground. I feel the life of the animal slip away and pull away. I sit back and wipe my mouth with my arm. I'm not alone, without even needing to smell, I know Drew is behind me. I turn slightly and see him sitting on his haunches as if waiting for me to finish. I stand up and back away from my kill dusting the snow from my body.

Drew moves toward my kill and sits next to it before looking at me. I stare back at him in confusion. He just sits there looking in my direction. Then it dawns on me. Wolves are scavengers, they will eat what has already been killed and they eat all of it. My stomach turns just a bit and I turn around finally understanding. I hear Drew snort just before he rips into the carcass on the ground.

The noises behind me finally cease. I slowly turn around to see Drew, as he finishes burying the remains of the carcass.

"How far away are we from where you wanted to go?" I ask him.

Drew walks over to me and shifts quickly. His shifting looks painful but he doesn't show that it is.

"Just over the next rise. Don't fret, you can rinse off when we get there." Drew says as he plucks some twigs from my hair.

I lean over near his ear. "You could use a good rinse yourself." I whisper and lightly lick the blood from his cheek.

I freeze. What did I do that for? A low rumbling sound comes from Drew. I backup, quickly keeping my eyes on him. He is so hard to read. I want to know what he is thinking. A muscle in Drew's jaw twitches. Say something. I plead silently.

"Let's go." Drew says. He shifts quickly and takes off running.

I sigh. Great. Just freaking great. Way to blow it moron, I berate myself. I run after him but follow him at a distance. I don't want him thinking I am desperately chasing after him. Not after that rejection!

I reach the top of the next rise but Drew is nowhere to be found. Below in a small valley is a long ranch style home. Soft glowing lights come from some of the windows, as if lit by candlelight. Behind the house is a small gazebo and just beyond that is a private lake. The view is obscenely gorgeous, even at night.

I follow the tracks Drew left in the snow down to the house where a side door is standing wide open. I tentatively take a step into the home, without Drew it feels like trespassing. The room appears to be a mudroom. It has wood paneled walls with matching hard wood flooring. Wooden coat racks matching the paneling are mounted onto the walls. It smells like old wood polish in here. Drew's boots sit by the door I just came through. I take off my boots and place them next to Drew's.

The smell of blood draws my attention, I quickly leave the mudroom and find myself in a large great room, every wall made of polished logs, even the ceiling and the support beams. The room is larger than my whole apartment that I had before this mess started! On a small table, across the room, is a wine glass full of deep red liquid. I move toward the table and find myself in front of it quickly. I scoop up the cup and take a drink. It isn't fresh but this is better than the animal I just had.

Another scent catches my attention and I look around for the source. On the floor are pink flower petals making a path to another room. Following the petal path I find myself in a smaller more intimate living room with plush white couches and floor to ceiling windows on one side. As I'm looking around Drew steps out from the kitchen that adjoins this room with his own wine glass. I look at him curiously.

"Yes, mine is actually wine." He chuckles.

"You did all this?" I ask, somewhat confused. His actions earlier made me think he was mad. That he wasn't into me. What was that all about if he did this?

"I had some help, but yes." He grins. "I thought you could use some of the real thing besides just the thrill of a hunt. Besides, watching you hunt is enjoyable. I still remember your first time."

I stifle a laugh. I remember. I performed a lovely face plant in the dirt for him missing an animal, came home dirty and covered in animal blood. We sit down on the couch, and place our glasses on the glass coffee table in front of us.

I look over at Drew. All of these mixed signals is messing with my mind. I have to know.

"What was that back there? Why did you seem irritated?" I ask him.

"When?" Drew asks, the confusion on his face obvious.

"After I, um, licked you. I didn't actually plan that. Your reaction to what I did wasn't expected either." I explain while looking down at my fingernails.

"Oh. Well if you must know. It was taking every ounce of control that I had, not to pounce on you right there. I wanted you to see the surprise that was waiting here. That is why I took off like that." Drew says with a slight sigh.

A hand lifts my face up and I find myself looking into Drew's gorgeous blue eyes. "I thought you knew how I felt about you. I have felt the same about you since I first met you, back in grade school. The one for me has only ever been you. Nothing, not even your recent alteration has changed that." A golden ring forms around his pupil as he talks.

Without another word, Drew's lips are on mine. His lips move over mine in a soft caress. I can feel a hunger building inside me and my fangs elongate. I quickly back away from Drew without saying anything.

"I'm sorry I shouldn't have just assumed you felt the same." Drew says apologetically.

"No, it isn't that. I do care and want this too." I say gesturing to the both of us. "It's just, is this normal?" I look up at him and point to my teeth.

Drew laughs. "Yes, I've seen that reaction on sexually excited Vampires before. When you're older you will have better control over when your fangs come out. The glow in your eyes, that doesn't fade with time, but blue looks good on you."

"My new set of teeth don't bother you?" I ask cautiously.

"Nope. It makes things a bit tricky, but nothing I'm not willing to work with. We will take it as slow as you need." He says.

"Oh." I grin. "I'm afraid I will want to take things slow. In fact, I think I want to take all night." I wink at him. "Just not here, I will feel a little too exposed come dawn." I giggle.

Drew flushes slightly and swallows hard as he catches my meaning.

CHAPTER 16

Rob

Morning sun light filters through the open air windows. The sitting room of my mother's suite is decorated in soft and warm hues of pink and green. Glow lamps float in the air, barely lit, adding to the soft, natural atmosphere my mother prefers. The smell of the cinnamon scones and tea on the table make my mouth water slightly. I sit down on one of the chairs across from the love seat my mother is currently perched on. I pick up a scone and place it on a plate, while my mother pours me a cup of tea. I fidget restlessly while waiting. Once she finishes, I pick up the cup and take a sip.

"What is troubling you so much? You cannot seem to sit still nor enjoy your breakfast with me." My mother looks at me curiously.

I set my teacup back down on the table beside me. I am not sure where to even start. I swallow my tea and blurt out the first thought on my mind. "It is Avalon. I fear for her safety."

"Why would you fear for her safety? Especially here, within the Sidhe. She is safest here." My mother scoffs.

"Is she? How much do we know about Oonagh's fosterling? Is he safe to be around her? I do not know much of anything about him except that he arrived shortly before Rion came here." I retort.

My mother chuckles softly. "Jealous are we? All this over competition?" My mother shakes her head. "Do not try to deny it. I see the way you look at her. I see the way she looks at you. It is not the same. Could it change with time? Possibly, but she must come to that choice on her own, my son."

"Do you know something about him that has not been disclosed to me?" I narrow my eyes at her. I caught the way she deflected my concerns about Braelomdrel to this being all about me.

"I may but it is not my information to disclose to you. Just know that Oonagh would not have a fosterling she did not trust." My mother looks back at me daring to question her further. "Is that all that has been troubling you?"

"No. The rest father needs to hear as well." I say softly. No sooner than the words are out, my father, Oberon walks into the room.

"What is it that I need to hear?" He asks, sitting down next to my mother on the love seat.

"I saw Kieran during my last trip to Colorado." I reply.

My mother gasps slightly. She never took well to Kieran leaving the Sidhe to live among the humans. My father pats her hand slightly and looks at me to continue.

"He was with Morcant. I saw him before Carl died and Avalon flooded the tunnels. I do not know if he survived the flood or if he escaped before it happened." My mother breaks down into sobs. "He could still be alive." I try to comfort her.

"My love, I think we would know if our youngest perished. Do you not believe this?" My father looks into my mother's eyes in earnest. She nods her head slightly.

"Is there any hope of saving him?" My father asks.

"I do not know. If we see him again, I will bring him home. We can try to see if he can be saved or not." I reply.

My father nods.

CHAPTER 17

Avalon

I softly knock on the polished wooden door to my grandmother's suite. I find it odd that my grandparents have separate suites. I suppose after being together this long, maybe it is a necessity.

A tall woman with long blond hair and ice blue eyes opens the door for me. "Princess Avalon, the Queen is waiting for you, please follow me." Without waiting for my acknowledgment, the woman turns around and walks farther into the suite. I quickly follow before the door closes on me. The room is lavishly decorated with gilded painted portraits, fine tapestries and unique sculptures. A soft cream color covers the walls, allowing the decor stand out. In the middle of the room is a love seat, two chairs (my grandmother in one) and a small table.

"Avalon. Do sit down with me?" My grandmother gestures to the peach and green chair beside her.

"Do you mind sharing breakfast with me?" She asks pointing out the tea and cakes sitting on the small wooden table beside her.

"No. I would be happy to. I want to get to know you better, but I have many questions." I reply, sitting down into the chair.

"I would be surprised if you did not." My grandmother chuckles softly as she pours the tea. "You were always an inquisitive child."

"About that." I pause for a moment while picking up a cake and plate. "I need you to clear something up for me." I say bluntly

"About what dear?" She looks at me with interest.

"How is it that I came to see you all those times as a child? Did you come to see me in the park? Or did I come here? Why did you not tell me of our connection?" I rattle off.

"Right down to it and direct, just like your mother." My grandmother sighs nostalgically. "I do not have the ability to travel between the realms. That ability appears to be yours. You appeared one day in my private gardens. I knew immediately who you were, but your mother wanted our world kept from you until adulthood. Frankly, I did not understand her reasons. I still do not, since children are more susceptible to magic. Perhaps, it was because of what we are. Maybe she was not ready for you to know."

"Rob explained that you are of the Tuatha De Danann.

Why should that matter so much?" I look at her in confusion while sipping the tea gingerly.

"How much did Rob explain?" She asks cautiously.

I caught the emphasis she used with Rob's name but put it from my mind for now. "He showed me how our people came to Ireland and then The Dagda separated our people from the world. Why?"

"Avalon there is much you do not know. That is why I must speak with you now before any other decisions are made." She says seriously.

"Okay." I reply warily, not sure if continuing to eat breakfast is a good idea.

"Before I can begin. Do you believe that God and Lucifer exist?" My grandmother asks before sipping her tea.

"Yes, but I don't see what they have to do with this." I say while putting down my plate and tea cup.

"They have everything to do with this." She says calmly. "When the world was young, there was a war in Heaven. This war was between God and his angels. Lucifer, whom God called his 'Morning Star', turned against him. Several angels followed Lucifer. Several angels did not join either side and watched. When God defeated Lucifer and his followers, they were sent to the bowels of the Earth."

I move to speak but my grandmother raises her hand for me to keep silent. I pick up the tea cup and begin sipping quietly while my grandmother continues her story.

"The angels that refused to choose a side were also banished from Heaven. Even though their individual gifts were not taken away, they could no longer enter into Heaven. They were told they would remain on Earth until the end of days." She stands up from her chair and walks towards the window.

"Those angels, the ones banished to Earth, are the Tuatha De Danann." She says as blinding white wings explode out from her back.

I choke and sputter, my tea cup and plate of cake fall to the floor. Nothing could have prepared me for this! I look back at my grandmother who looks at me in concern. I hold a hand out, gesturing that I'm fine. Only I'm not really fine. All the stories that were told at church as a kid, they aren't just stories! I think I'm going to be sick.

"I'm half angel?" I ask incredulously.

"You are." My grandmother confirms.

"Okay, maybe now I can see why my mom wanted the secret kept. This is the biggest whammy of all." I say.

"There is more that you must know." She says softly.

"More?" My voice raises an octave.

"If you decide to go through the Awakening, I cannot keep this secret. By going through the Awakening, you accept all of your heritage, including the burdens of each race I fear."

"What burdens?" I ask in alarm.

"It is believed, that because of our inactions, there is no hope for salvation for the Angels on Earth. No one knows if this is true of our offspring. Since you are not a full Angel, this doesn't apply now. If you go through the Awakening, it could." She says gravely.

I stare dumbly at her. This is so much to take in.

"The Awakening Ceremony can be scary at first, but no one there wishes any other harm. Once you have accepted, no one can assist you until it is finished. You will have to work your way back to us on your own." Oonagh advises.

"Couldn't be more cryptic could you?" I mutter and roll my eyes.

"It is really all I can tell you. The experience for everyone is different. That I can recall, no one that has gone through the Awakening in the Sidhe has been of more than two bloodlines, with human always being the other. I have no idea what you will experience." Oonagh explains, a look of worry shows on her face.

What else will I have to do for these people? Is there anything more they will require of me before this is done?

"One more thing you need to know." Oonagh says, interrupting my thoughts.

I sigh.

"By going through the Awakening and accepting your place as the Heir, you must go to the Stone. The large pillar that stands near the thrones in the Great Hall. It is one of our oldest treasures. If it sings for you, it tells the people you are the rightful and true Heir to the throne." Oonagh says.

"What if it doesn't sing?" I ask.

"It will. Of that I have no doubt, my dear." Oonagh smiles.

"When am I supposed to make my decision by?" I ask quietly.

"As soon as possible. The longer you wait, the more powerful Morcant and his people become." She says solemnly.

I nod. "I have another question. The water that is used in the Awakening, it isn't ordinary water. What is it?"

"The water is not what you think it is. The Dagda's cauldron, that he had with him at all times, contained the tears of his heartbreak."

"How do drinking tears put someone through an Awakening?" I ask incredulously. The thought of drinking some old dude's tears is rather gross.

"I am not sure. It was a side effect we learned of years ago. When the first of us started to have offspring, most were of mixed parentage with humans, as pure angel offspring are extremely rare. Most of the offspring, even the ones of mixed blood, were sickly and weak. Some swapped those children with healthy human ones, even though the replacements were never really brought up as one of the blood would have been. One new mother was adamant that she would not swap her child and was desperate to find something that would cure him. She sought the advice of the Dagda. When the little boy seemed interested in his cauldron, the Dagda was kind to him and allowed him a closer look. When the Dagda was consulting with the mother, the boy fell into the cauldron. When he was lifted out, he started to glow and then wings grew out of his back. When the young boy opened his eyes once more, his eyes were like ours, tri-colored. After that, experiments were done with the water from the cauldron."

"The Weres." I state quietly.

"Yes, your friend, his ancestors were a part of the experiment. Since that first boy, we have waited Awakening our mixed children and even the rare pure children. We wait until they are 18, and can make the decision on their own." She says solemnly.

"Is that boy still here?" I ask.

My grandmother nods. "I assume you would like to talk to him?" She inquires.

"Yes."

"Zephyr is the one you need to talk to. I know you have many things to do today. You have many things to think about and decide upon. You may go, but feel free to come see me any time." My grandmother says.

I stand up, clearly dismissed. I walk towards the door without looking back, thinking over the morning's revelations.

~*~

I walk through the Palace looking for Zephyr. I haven't

the faintest idea where he could be. Everyone seems so healthy here. Rob never showed me where the medical facility is. I wonder if there is one. I come across a young maid carrying linens.

"Excuse me. Do you know where I can find Zephyr?" I ask her.

The maid drops into an immediate curtsy. "He is normally in the gardens at this time collecting herbs." The girl says meekly.

Something about her mannerisms bug me. As if she is afraid of me. I don't like it.

"Please stand up. I will not hurt you." I say softly. "I do not know what you are used to here, but I'm not like that."

The maid stands up and nods, but doesn't move. I realize she is waiting for me to dismiss her. It will take some time for me to get used to this way of life.

"You may go." I say and continue on to the gardens.

I reach the paned doors and walk out into the morning sunlight that filters through the leaves of the trees. I scan the garden and its walkways looking for Zephyr. I hear someone humming a tune from the party. Following the sound, I find Zephyr at the edge of the gardens harvesting lavender.

"What can I do for you Princess?" Zephyr asks without looking to see who is behind him.

"How did you know it was me?" I ask curiously.

"You have a certain gait, like your brother, but not so

heavy. The other Sidhe do not walk as the two of you do." Zephyr explains.

I feel as if he just said I'd sounded like an elephant walking.

"I wanted to talk to you about something rather personal, if you wouldn't mind." I say softly.

"Your grandmother mentioned as much. She is another reason I knew you were on your way." Zephyr chuckles for a moment. "What would you like to know?"

"The Awakening. What was it like? Do you believe you are condemned to your parents' fate even though you didn't get a choice?"

Zephyr's eyes widen. "You surely do not beat around the bush. Straight to the point. I like that. Well, since I was not very old when it happened, I cannot tell you what it was like. I remember being very sick, weak and almost always in pain. Then one day I was healthy and strong."

I nod.

"I do not feel condemned to the fate of my parents. If I am, then God would not be a just God in my eyes. I cannot live my life thinking that way either. You only live once. You must live your life in the best way possible." Zephyr says solemnly.

"Thank you. Talking to someone else with the same lineage helps bring things into perspective." I say with a smile.

Zephyr nods and goes back to harvesting lavender. I turn and walk back toward the palace.

CHAPTER 18

Nickolai

The cool night air blows through the barracks, creating a whistling noise through the planks of the walls. I lay down on my bunk, exhausted from the day's training. My muscles burn and I need to rest, there is no telling when Senna will spring a surprise training session. We have been in the Sidhe for a week now. I let my mind wander, and wonder what Avalon is doing.

Since the day we arrived at the Palace, I was quickly removed from her presence. I have gotten to see her once. It was more of a glance really. I wonder if she even remembers that I'm here. The night of the party, she seemed so wrapped up with the guy from the Great Hall. The look I saw in Rob's face that night, makes me think she has forgotten about him too.

My stomach rumbles in protest, I can't remember the last time I ate. I roll over onto my side and twist to reach under the bunk. The backpack is on its side looking rather empty. I grab the backpack and bring it up to me as I roll back over onto my back. Quickly, I open the pack and rummage through my supplies. I start to count my rations. My time here is almost up.

I'm grateful for the additional training that Senna has given me. By far, that has been the most helpful since I have learned more about my capabilities and abilities here than anywhere. Sparring with races here that I didn't even know existed, has pushed me to my limits.

What am I really doing here anyway? The only reason I came along in the first place was for Avalon. It is clear I'm not needed, at least not for the reason I was hoping to be. I have learned a lot about myself and my abilities here, but that is all. I haven't enjoyed myself here. This is Avalon's world, not mine. I can help the cause against Morcant better back home, organizing our forces and training others with the techniques learned here.

A knock raps against the wooden door frame of the barrack entrance. I look over and spot Rion standing in the doorway.

"Hey." Rion says.

"Hey. What's up?" I reply.

"I wanted to check up on you and see the status of your rations." Rion states as he steps inside the barracks.

"How is Avalon?" I blurt out.

Rion sighs. "Avalon is being put through the ringer right

now. Between training, family history and other royal duties she hasn't had time for much. Her only fun time was the party last night. She has been as busy as you. To be frank, I don't see where she will have much time to visit with you. Is she the only reason you are here?" He asks and stretches his hand out for my backpack.

I hand him my backpack. "For the most part, I was only able to join her here because of the circumstances surrounding your father's death. I have learned so much here. I think my time here is almost up. It is time I return and do what can be done back home."

Rion nods. "You are correct. The combat maneuvers and strategies you have learned here will be best taught to others that want to help. I will let the council know of your supply situation. You should be going home with Rob tomorrow."

Rion walks back to the doorway and then turns around.

"If you would like to leave a note for my sister, there are writing supplies in the desk." Rion points to the desk on the far end of the barracks. "I will make sure that she gets it."

CHAPTER 19

Avalon

Light filters through my bedroom window. The birds chirping and squirrels racing through the tree branches outside the window make me feel as if it is spring. The information my grandmother imparted to me the day before still swirls in my head. I open my eyes slowly, finding breakfast on the table, along with coffee this time from the smell. Tea just doesn't cut it in the morning, not enough caffeine!

I get out of bed finding my clothes laid out for the day. Cotton shirt, pants and socks lay at the foot of the bed with my sneakers on the floor. Yes! No formal wear. It also means I have training today. I change into my clothes and sit down to eat breakfast. Waffles and eggs. Totally yum! I squeal with delight.

Amberley comes into the room picks up my night clothes and giggles slightly. "Excitement over waffles and eggs? Oh, your escort will be here shortly to take you to your training lessons." She reminds me.

I cram in my breakfast and wash it down with orange juice. Jumping up from the table, I run to the bathroom. I squeeze some toothpaste on my toothbrush and barely run it under the water before shoving it in my mouth and brush briskly. I spit hastily in the sink, rinse my mouth, and dash out to the sitting room.

Amberley laughs. "You had more time than that. Dashing about like a mad woman was not necessary."

I grin back. "Sorry, I'm just excited to learn more about what I can do. Apparently, I have more abilities that I need to learn to control. Some, I have no idea how to use or the extent of them."

Amberley nods. "It is best that you learn to control and how far you should go with them."

I notice the look in her eyes when she says the last part. I wonder what she knows. Amberley doesn't say anything further and walks out of the room, leaving me alone with my thoughts.

I sit down on the couch and fidget with my hair, thinking back to all that has transpired since I have arrived. I hope one of my training sessions today deals with the dreams that I have been having. The first ones have worked themselves out but the new one, the first night in the Sidhe, I'm not sure what all of that was about. Why did Braelomdrel's face keep changing? Does he have something to do with my future or am I just reading more into these dreams than I should? I mean, he is HOT!

I wish there was someone that I could talk to freely. After the party and seeing Rob's face, I don't think he would like me to discuss my dreams and how hot I think Braelomdrel is. I haven't seen him since the party. I know he feels more for me than I do for him. It isn't that I don't like him, I do, just not the way he wants.

There is this thing with Braelomdrel that is hard to resist. I just don't know what I want. Getting into a relationship right now might not be the best idea either, since my future is up in the air right now. It wouldn't be fair to the one I become involved with if something should happen.

Grandmother's revelation yesterday only compounds everything. I grew up thinking that when I die, that I would go to heaven. Yet, if I choose to embrace my heritage, that all goes away? What would happen to me if I died? It is a scary thought. If I don't accept the Awakening though, what happens to everyone else? No pressure!

A rapping noise on the door brings me out of my thoughts. Amberley opens the door and Rion walks in.

"Ready for the fun to begin?" He asks with a sparkle in his eyes.

"Rion, I have a question first." I reply.

"What is troubling you? I can see it in your face." He walks over and sits down with me. "Whatever it is, you can talk to me. Just like we used to."

"Have you gone through the Awakening yet? Do you

know everything about where we come from?" I blurt out.

"I do know where we come from, Grandmother told me a few days after my arrival. She doesn't believe in keeping secrets from us Avalon. As for the Awakening, I haven't gone through that yet. I was ready at one point recently, but with what happened with Dad and his change, it was recommended that I wait. Dad almost didn't make it through his change because he was Were and Merrow. We are more, the Awakening will be hard for us. To be honest, it kind of scares me." He explains.

"Oh." My voice trails off. I hadn't known what Dad had gone through to help save me. I didn't know he almost died in the process. Rion and I have more than one blood line, from what I heard in the council room we have four. I feel sick.

"I shouldn't have said that right before training. I'm sorry. Okay, change of subject. Instead of dwelling on that crap. Think of all the cool stuff you are going to learn." He grins at me.

I grin back. "So which one is first?"

"First up, is Water training. They want to test your abilities to see where you are at in your control. From Rob's reports it is quite powerful, even without being fully Awakened. After that I will check with the other teachers to see who is ready for you." He replies.

"Let's go then." I say, standing up from the couch.

~*~

"Again!" Maridine commands.

I quickly pull water from the cove, shaping it into various forms, freezing and sending my ice weapons sailing across the cove only to make them rapidly heat up into vapor before hitting a poor Merrow that was to be my living target. I had already grazed him once by not being fast enough.

"Good. Now this time, do not pull the water from the cove." Maridine says with a smile.

"How does that work?" I ask.

"Think child. Look at your surroundings and what they are composed of. If the obvious water source isn't available you need to find it elsewhere. The air around you, the plants." Maridine stopped short as if catching herself from saying something. "Look deep beneath the earth where water flows in the hidden waterways. If you cannot find enough from one source, use multiple sources!"

I nod. I begin looking for water in the ways that she says, after a bit I can feel the water's call. Drawing the water to me, I can see the sources it comes from, the nearby trees and other plants as well as the air around me. I repeat the exercise.

"Very good. There is nothing more that I can teach you." Maridine says.

"Thank you for spending time out of your schedule to teach me." I reply.

For some reason, it feels like there is more to learn. I don't know why that is or if there is why Maridine claims there is no more to teach.

"We are family. You will make us proud!" Maridine smiles warmly and then looks past beyond my shoulder. "You need to come see us soon, my boy, we need to work on your skills, they are lacking!"

I look back and see Rion grinning sheepishly. "I will." Rion replies.

"So what is next?" I ask.

"Well, both of them are ready for you so it is your choice. You can work on your vision thing or your gate ability." He says.

Slowly a melody begins to play in the air. I look around for its source. There are no Merrows about any more. I have no idea where it is coming from. Rion looks at me quizzically.

"You don't hear that?" I question him.

"Hear what exactly?" He raises an eyebrow at me.

"You don't hear the music?" I look incredulously at him.

"Uh, no. Do you often hear things no one else does since your abilities have surfaced? Maybe it is something related to your dreaming, vision thing. I think it might be best to visit with the teacher for that now." He looks at me a bit weird but concerned.

~*~

Rion stops in front of a grassy hill, a door made of leather hangs over the opening. Little puffs of smoke escape from behind the leather.

"Aislinn, I have Avalon with me, she is here for training." Rion calls out.

I wait patiently. Faint clattering noises come from behind the leather hanging. The leather is pulled aside and a red haired, matronly woman beckons me inside.

"I will be back later." Rion says and gestures for me to go inside.

"Please sit down and get comfortable. I apologize for the incense, it may be a bit overwhelming at first." Aislinn smiles sweetly and continues on. "From what I have been told, you have the gift of the sight but only while sleeping?"

I nod as I sit down. The room we are in, if you can call it a room, is bathed in soft candle light. Candles in white, blue and purple provide light for this space.

"Sometimes a physical manifestation appears as well?" She inquires.

I nod again.

"Interesting." She mutters as she settles herself into the big cushion next to mine.

"First off, we will start with a guided meditation and see what you get from that. Any questions you have that are not answered with your assessment today can be asked before

Rion comes. Alright?" She looks at me waiting for my acknowledgment.

"Okay." I say. The incense is rather overpowering, but the atmosphere is relaxing.

"I want you to sit up straight and breathe in deep for a count of four. Then you are to hold your breath for a count of four, and finally release for a count of four. Repeat this cycle at least 20 times." Aislinn says firmly.

Aislinn continues to talk in a slow, soothing rhythm. I lose track of the cycles after a while and feel almost as if I'm floating.

Slowly a white light forms in my vision, even though my eyes are closed. I focus on the light and it grows bigger. Suddenly a large eye is looking at me. Around the semi-slitted pupil is a gleaming gold color that fades into a mossy green, followed by a deep grey-blue color. I gasp. Those eyes, they are the ones I saw in my dream.

"What do you see?" Aislinn probes.

"An eye." I hear myself say quietly, without the excitement I really feel.

"An eye?" Aislinn repeats incredulously. "Describe it."

I describe the eye that I continue to look at. It blinks, quickly changing back to a white orb, then back again to the depths of the sun on the sea.

"Clear it from your mind. Will it away and go back to the darkness." Aislinn commands.

I try to do as she says. The eye wavers for a moment and then seems to appear more solid. The melody I heard at the cove sounds again before everything goes black. I sit up in shock. What was that?

"What happened? We weren't finished." Aislinn demands.

"I was trying to do as you said. The eye that I saw wavered just for a moment and then was even more prominent than before. Then I heard a song, the same song that I've heard twice now, but this time it was faint." I explain.

"You have been hearing things no one else can hear? A song?" Aislinn questions me.

I nod. "Is it related to the sight?" I inquire.

"Perhaps." Aislinn says but appears deep in thought. She looks directly into my eyes this time. "Tell me what you have seen since you have arrived."

I describe the dream I had the first night in the Sidhe. Her eyes narrow but then she nods.

"Does the dream mean that I'm supposed to be with Braelomdrel?" I ask softly.

Aislinn laughs. "No child. It only means that he is involved with your future, not that you and he will or should be 'together' as you kids put it. You read too much into it Avalon. Did you think you and the Prince were destined to be together after you dreamt of him?"

"I did at first." I admitted, blushing in embarrassment.

"Now you do not believe this to be true?" Aislinn asks quietly.

"Due to surrounding circumstances, it feels a bit weird. I mean, I like him. I just don't know that we'd be best suited for each other." I explain quickly.

"You would know better than any other." Aislinn smiles warmly at me. "You have managed to have a vision while awake, though its meaning is unclear at this juncture. Keep practicing your meditation daily and see what comes of it. Do not let these visions overtake you while asleep, they can become too powerful if they have to push into your consciousness when you are vulnerable." She warns me.

I nod.

"Do you have any questions before you go?" Aislinn asks as she stands up from her cushion.

"No, I think my questions for the most part have been answered." I reply and make my way toward the doorway.

"Feel free to come see me if you have additional visions like the first. We will examine it together and try to determine if there is a proper course to take from that." Aislinn calls out.

I walk out into the sunlight and quickly shield my eyes from the harsh light.

"Ready?" Rion says.

I nod. I can't see him clearly so I extend my hand out for

guidance and he takes it.

He places paper in my hand. "Read this after your next lesson. You can't be distracted during lessons involving gateways, I've heard you have to maintain focus." He says quietly.

~*~

Rion escorts me to a small, heavily wooded enclosure. In the middle of it stands a tall, tanned man with many tattoos.

"Bain!" I call out excitedly and stuff the paper in my hand into my pocket.

Bain turns and smiles brightly at me then nods to Rion. At times like these, I feel like the little sister instead of the oldest sibling.

"It is good to see you again Princess." Bain says.

The low, guttural tone of his voice isn't what makes me stop walking toward him. My mouth opens in shock. He talks!

Bain lets out a low, rumbling laugh. "I can talk, but I know you cannot communicate with me through my preferred method of mindspeak."

I nod. That method sounds neat and frustrates me just a little.

"Since you have not demonstrated this ability for many years, we will start off small. I want you to focus in your mind's eye a place you know well. Your sitting room, the garden, anywhere within the Sidhe." Bain instructs. "If you need to, meditate to clear you mind and then focus on your place of interest. See it clearly in your mind. When you are ready, stand up and walk." He says as he takes my hand.

I sit down slowly and begin the breathing techniques Aislinn showed me earlier. When my mind is free of clutter, I focus on the Great Hall at the top of the dais, near the High thrones of the Sidhe. I have only been in the room once. This would be easier if I had an eidetic memory.

With my destination in place, I stand up slowly and feel Bain's weight shift in my hand. I walk forward and the sounds of the enclosure are replaced with gasps.

I open my eyes to see us on the dais of the Great Hall, in front of my grandfather. He has a look of fury on his face. He looks to Bain. There's the wordless exchange again. I can tell by the pensive look on their faces.

"Out loud!" I demand. Looking them both square in the face, my jaw set and fists clenched.

With a roll of his eyes my grandfather looks at me. "Alright, I will ask you. What are you doing in here? You were not summoned." My grandfather says in an exasperated tone.

His tone puts my back up. "Training. It wasn't Bain's idea, but mine." I look around the room. It is deserted, except for a few scantily clad women seated on the steps.

I snort. "I did not mean you interrupt your 'entertainment'." I choke back a laugh. Now I know why Grandmother has her own room. What a pig.

"You will not come into my presence unless summoned, is that clear?" My grandfather rages at me.

The same oily feeling comes over me as it did in the council chambers. I squirm slightly. I don't know what that is but I don't like it. I look up at him. "I have more important things to do and as you can see, I don't need to be summoned. I can come and go as I please." I challenge him.

He looks taken aback, as if not used to being challenged and not getting his way. Before he can say another slimy word I take Bain's hand and walk.

Suddenly I'm back in the enclosure. Bain lets out the loudest belly laugh I have ever heard. I turn to look at him.

"I have never seen anyone do what you just did." Bain says through his laughter. "Not only do you pull a ballsy move but his words have no effect on you. It was a priceless moment I will never forget."

I grin.

"You did very well for your first try. The same concept applies when going through the veil between the Sidhe and your Earth. If you go blindly without a thought in mind but just to escape, that will not be good for one with your abilities." He warns.

"Why would it be bad?" I ask.

"You could end up anywhere, especially after you go through your Awakening. Your abilities are already strong. Once you are Awakened, I do not know if you will be one of the rare ones that can go other places." Bain's voice drifted off.

"Other places?" I look at him in astonishment.

"I am just speculating. You could end up at the bottom of the ocean, or in the middle of a jungle somewhere." Bain quickly corrects himself and then gets a pensive look on his face again. "Sorry to cut this short, but I am needed elsewhere, practice transporting yourself around the Sidhe, do not attempt transport back to Earth just now. Please transport yourself to your sitting room, the Prince is busy elsewhere and unable to escort you."

~*~

I step into my sitting room, startling Amberley out of the chair she is sitting in.

"Princess!" Amberley squeaks in alarm. "How? Where is Prince Rion?"

I giggle softly. "Rion is busy doing something else, I was told to come back here since he couldn't escort me."

"You traveled on your own?" Amberley says, her eyes wide in astonishment.

"I transported myself here, yes. I'm sure word will get out soon of what happened today anyway." I snicker to myself.

"What did you do? That impish look on your face tells me it could not have been good." Amberley looks at me.

I can't tell if Amberley is trying to be stern or just trying not to join me in my giggles. I explain what happened in the Great Hall during my training.

A swift exhale escapes her and she doubles over laughing. "Oh to have been a butterfly on that wall!" Amberley manages to get out between fits of giggles.

I put my hands in my pockets out of habit and feel the paper that had been hastily shoved into it. I pull it out of my pocket carefully, walk over to the couch and sit down. Unfolding the paper I see that it is a note of some kind. Amberley quietly excuses herself from the room as I sit back to read the note.

Avalon,

I hope that you have found your happiness here, with family. I have not seen you since we arrived at the Palace, I don't know how things are with you or how things stand between us. Not that I believe there is an "us" any longer, but I do hope we are at least friends. I have learned so much here. You are truly in good hands. I hope to see you again one day to catch up. When you read this, I will already be back in Colorado with Rob. You will make a hell of a ruler one day, I believe that. Don't let that nasty grandfather of yours push you around. If you choose to go through the Awakening and help save us from Morcant and his followers, he will be greatly indebted to you. Remember that!

Always,

Nickolai

Oh my gosh! I completely forgot about Nickolai. Amberley comes into the room with a tray of tea and cakes. My stomach wants to rebel. I feel horrible. How could I have ignored him like that? I should have at least gone to see him while he was still here. I look back at the letter. Nickolai's faith in me and his support mean so much, even though there is no "us", he is right on that, I would still like to have him as my friend. Besides, if I'm to rule the Sidhe one day it will also be important to have contacts on Earth. No matter how I try to justify it, I'm still feeling horrible about what I've done. I have a feeling I will see him again though.

CHAPTER 20

Rob

Closing the door to my suite, I turn and almost walk over the top of a young elfin boy in palace livery. I bend over and help the lad from the floor, checking to make sure he is not injured.

"I am sorry your Highness. I was sent to give you a message to come to the council chambers for a meeting." The young elf stated nervously.

I nod in acknowledgment and wave him off to assume is regular duties. There is no council meeting scheduled today that I am aware of. Curious, I make my way to the council chambers. The sun shines brightly through the windows, rendering the glow globes useless but still floating mid-air. I reach the council chambers and a guard opens the door for me as I approach. Without sparing him a glance, I walk into the room.

The room is almost deserted save for small gathering of people. The glow globes are dimly lit and centered around the gathered group. Not the usual council meeting. Nickolai is standing with Rion next to Oonagh and Braelomdrel. Finvarra and my parents are also gathered near the front of the room. It must be time for Nickolai to go back to Colorado. I knew he didn't have enough rations in his backpack to stay very long. I hope he learned much in his time here.

"Time to take you home then?" I ask.

Nickolai nods and adjusts the small, almost empty pack on his shoulder. He looks at me expectantly. Why?

"Nickolai must be taken back home. Being well versed in the situation it has been decided that you will join him." Braelomdrel states swiftly.

My eyes narrow. I know what he is doing. Getting rid of the competition. I clench my teeth and try to keep my hands from tightening into fists.

"You will be our liaison, between Earth and the Sidhe. We need you to help coordinate everyone there while we get the Princess and all who wish to join her ready." Braelomdrel continues.

I look to my parents, Finvarra and Oonagh. They all nod in agreement. It is done then, I do not have recourse when they all agree.

"When do we go and what gate will be used?" I ask of no one in particular.

"We may go whenever you are ready." Bain says.

His voice startles me so much I actually break my stance. Rion, unfazed, walks over to me and whispers, "You are free to use all of my stuff just like before."

I nod. "I do not like this one bit. He just wants me gone so that your sister can be his." I spit out, albeit quietly.

Rion snorts. "My sister can take care of herself. She does not like anyone telling her she has to do anything. Avalon will decide for herself who she will be with, whether that be Braelomdrel, you or someone else entirely." Rion's voice takes on a serious note as he ends the conversation, obviously pointing to the fact that I am getting close to overstepping.

"Bain how do we get back to the house quickly?" I turn to ask.

"Easy. I will take you directly there. You know the place well enough. Just picture it in your mind and show me so I can focus on that." Bain replies.

I stand to the right of Bain and direct Nickolai to stand on the other side of him. I picture Carl's living room in my mind. I do not want to just instantly appear in the backyard, if anyone happens to be about there will be awkward questions. Startling Melanie and Drew are the least of my concerns. I project the image to Bain. He grips my shoulder and I close my eyes. I hate traveling, having your eyes open during it is nauseating.

Shouts and a multitude of running feet assault my ears. I open my eyes and look around quickly to discover eleven

Vampires heading straight for us, nails extended and fangs barred.

CHAPTER 21

Melanie

The atmosphere in the kitchen grew cold somehow. I look around me to see what's going on and see Rob, Nikolai and a large tattooed dude standing in the living room. A number of the Vampires are closing in on their location, their intentions obvious.

"Stop!" I yell, and eleven Vampires abruptly halt their advance on the trio in the living room.

"Rob, Nikolai. I'm glad you're back, where is Avalon?" I ask.

"Avalon is still in the Sidhe, learning how to fulfill her duties." Rob replies.

"It's true then? She is the daughter of the prophecy?" I question.

"Most likely. She is also the heir to the high throne of the

138

Sidhe." Nikolai states.

I stare at Nikolai and Rob in disbelief. The other Vampires leave the room, knowing we will share information they need to know later.

"Close your mouth, you may catch flies." Drew says to me with a laugh. "Glad you're back. I could use the help whipping this motley crew into shape." Drew fist bumps Nikolai.

I shoot a dirty look at Drew. He smiles and winks back at me. I screw up my face at him before realizing I was being watched. I quickly change direction.

"Who is your friend?" I inquire, turning back to Rob.

"Oh. I am sorry. That was extremely rude of me." Rob replies. "This is Bain, our official gatekeeper."

Bain gives a small nod.

"Oh. Is there more than one?" I ask with interest.

"Yes and no." Rob states curtly.

Bain looks over at Rob with an intense expression on his face. Rob nods.

"I must be going now." Bain says.

"Would you like something to eat or something to drink before you go?" I ask.

Bain shakes his head, and disappears. My jaw drops again and Drew leans over to help me close my mouth, chuckling.

"Would either of you care to explain why there are so many new Vampires in this house and how they have this much control? I thought you were an exception Melanie. How is it that there are over twenty with control in less than two weeks?" Nickolai asks quickly.

"Man, you have been gone eight months. It took Melanie almost two months to get most of them under control. Well, enough to get them here anyway." Drew replies.

"What?" Nickolai asks in astonishment, looking first at Drew then me.

"Time moves differently in the Sidhe. Why else do you think we look so young?" Rob quips.

I walk over and sit on the couch. The others follow me and take their seats.

"When I left you guys at the hotel, I went back to the mine for more blood bags. I was grabbing the bags and stuffing them into a pack that I'd found hanging on the wall when I heard these Vampires. Listening to their cries and voices I found them in the one of the back rooms. Nikolai there were about twenty-five of them. I couldn't just leave them there to starve and die. So I used the techniques you taught me and trained them." I explain.

"Where is everyone staying? Surely they haven't all been camping out in the basement for eight months!" Nickolai asks.

"Yes and no." I replied with a grin.

"We made use of their strength and speed during their

awake and coherent hours." Drew grins. "We've made some additional substructures. Some of the rooms and corridors extend out below the field out back."

Rob and Nickolai's eyes open wide in surprise.

"There is enough room for more. Besides, we can always make more room if needed." Drew smirks.

"So what is the plan now? What is really going on in the Sidhe?" I question and Nickolai looks at Rob for the answer.

"The plan is to train you all up to par, and then go from there. I will also send word to my scouts, to see if there may be others out in the world that are interested in joining us. Nickolai, you know of any others that would join us?" Rob asks Nickolai.

"None that I trust implicitly. If I contact others, they may give our position away." Nickolai replies quickly.

"As for what is going on in the Sidhe, there is little that I can divulge at this time. Avalon is learning how to better control and use her skills that she has. She also has a big decision to make, that will affect us all. That is all I can tell you." Rob states.

"What big decision?" I ask in confusion.

"Avalon must choose to go through the Awakening or not." Rob says.

"I thought she had already gone through that, even though there was no choice." I say.

"When I was here last do you remember how much

'water' I gave to Carl and Nickolai?" Rob asks me.

I nod.

"The vial that Nickolai had was the same amount that we use in our Awakening ceremony for one person. Avalon had only a drop and that was just enough to awaken her abilities." Rob informs us.

"You mean to tell me, what she was able to do at the mines, that was just a touch of her power?" I asked incredulously.

"I do not know." Rob answers with uncertainty.

CHAPTER 22

Braelomdrel

Today will hopefully be the day. Avalon has been so busy, is been hard to get close to her. With Rob in the other man she brought along with her gone, she will be alone. The time is ripe. I just need to talk to someone first.

I walk the long corridor in the early morning. The cross breeze keeps the corridor clean and refreshing, while birdsong floats through the air. I stop and knock on the door Oonagh's suite. The door opens and Caileen's no-nonsense demeanor suddenly shifts. Her face lights up and a wide smile greets me. She is a beautiful woman, and were it not for Avalon and Caileen's station, she might have been worth pursuing.

"Welcome, my dear. Do sit down with me?" Oonagh asks graciously as she points to the spot beside her. She looks at me for a moment and then nods. "Out with it, I know there is something on your mind."

"I am just not sure you would approve..." I start.

"What exactly needs my approval? You have never needed it before." Oonagh replies.

"I would like to start the courting process with Avalon." I blurt out.

Oonagh looks at me thoughtfully and then her eyes narrow. "Is this what you want or what your mother wants?"

"A bit of both." I reply sheepishly as my left hand runs through the back of my hair.

"I see. I love your mother, but I will not let her dictate the path for Avalon. Make sure your heart is in this before you go too far. I do not want her hurt more than what I know is coming already." She says solemnly.

I nodded in understanding and stand up.

"By the way, do not let Avalon know of your mother and her involvement in this. Also, do not let her know that you have initiated a courtship with her. Courtship is such an old fashioned term to Avalon, she may not accept you so willingly. To be honest, I think your mother has a rude awakening coming for her if she thinks my granddaughter will be pliable to her whims." Oonagh says and chuckles softly.

I smile, knowing she is probably right and excuse myself from her suite.

I close the door behind me and start off to find Arian. He always seems to know what all women want without actually knowing them. I want everything to be perfect for this afternoon and evening. My thoughts wander and I grin at all the possibilities that tonight might bring. Finally, after searching most of the palace and the courtyard, I find him meditating in the garden near a small fountain.

"Braelomdrel, it has been a while since you have sought me out. I take it a certain young lady has caught your eye?" Arian says in amusement without opening his eyes or straying from the meditative posture he is in.

How he can know who is within his presence and know exactly what they are after? It always takes me back a little. "It is uncanny how you do that. Yes, there is a certain someone." I reply.

"Ha! A princess, I would bet." Adrian grins. "You will need to take your time with that one. She is not one to trifle with. Do not toy with her affections either. If from what I have seen of her holds true, you will regret it." He warns.

"Have you been talking to Oonagh? She just said something similar." I look at him in surprise.

"We just know you well. You are of fine lineage and caliber, there is no doubt. Many women want you for their own. I am sure you have seen that for yourself. However, our Princess is different. She cares little for lineage, but holds character and honor in high regard. This young woman is like no other in the Sidhe from what I have seen and witnessed." Arian says outright.

"Is that a good or bad thing?" I ask him.

"I think it is a good change, a breath of fresh air for our

people. She will change many things as a ruler. Have you seen how she reacts to Finvarra? They are like oil and water, those two. She doesn't take his word at face value like everyone else seems to. I think taking things slow will also give you a chance to see for yourself if she is the right match." Arian confesses.

"What do you mean like everyone else seems to?" I ask in confusion.

Arian sighs. "There are a few of us, and I would bet our Princess is one too, that feel the power of coercion from Finvarra come over us and it rolls over our skin like a foul oil. If you can be sneaky about it, try a Draught of Truth sometime in your ale next time when in a discussion with him. You will see what I mean, when suddenly everyone starts to agree with him when just moments before they were not. Be careful, however, what secrets you share." Adrian says in warning.

"My secrets?" I ask, worried that he may have found me out in his uncanny way.

"Everyone has secrets, my boy. No, I do not know yours specifically so you can stop holding your breath now." Arian snickers.

"So how do you suggest I go about pursing and getting to know her better?" I ask him.

"Take the afternoon, have a picnic, and go for a swim. There is a nice place over near the falls. I will have the staff prepare a basket and set it out for you both there on a blanket. I will also have them bring extra towels for your swim." Arian says swiftly.

I nod and thank him. Walking back to my suite I think about all the things that need to be done before this afternoon, such as inviting Avalon. I enter my suite, sit down at my writing table, and take out a sheet of parchment and a quill. I jot down a quick invitation to Avalon and send it along with my valet, Arlin, to deliver it.

~*~

Freshly showered and dressed I sit waiting in my sitting room for a response from Avalon. It has been almost an hour, why is there no response yet to my invitation? The door opens and I stand up in anticipation. Arlin closes the door behind him.

"Well, what is the answer?" I ask hastily.

"It would not be proper to read your correspondence." Arlin replies taken a back that I would think such of him.

"Sorry Arlin, I do not know what came over me. Of course you would not do that." I apologize.

Arlin hands me a note baring the Seal of the Heir. I take it from him quickly, thank him and sit down, breaking the seal and opening the letter. The writing within is not in the fashion of the Sidhe and I sit there trying to read through her words.

Braelomdrel,

I'm happy to have received your invitation for this afternoon. I'll be ready within an hour. I look forward to talking with you some more. I want to learn more about the Sidhe through your perspective and not a stuffy, windbag politician.

See you soon,

Avalon

A stuffy, windbag politician? I laugh. Surely she is not calling me a stuffy windbag. I am not sure what that a stuffy windbag is, but it does not sound like a good thing. Her speech is so different and refreshing, even if I do not catch half of the meaning behind it. I did not think it was possible, but I am looking forward to this afternoon with more excitement than before.

~*~

I stand out in the courtyard and wait for Avalon. I try not to bounce on the balls of my feet out of nervousness. At the sounds of light footsteps on the stone walkway, I turn. Avalon smiles sweetly but her clothes make me want to rip off mine. Her light blue, airy sun-dress with thin straps clings to her curves. The sunlight makes the dress a tad see through. The delicate sandals on her small feet shows off her perfectly polished nails.

"Hi!" Avalon says brightly. "I haven't made you wait long, right?"

I smile. "No, I have not been waiting long." Just all day, I think to myself.

"So where are we off to?" She asks.

Unable to grasp her meaning, I look at her in confusion.

"Oh, sorry." She apologizes quickly. "I mean, where are we going? Is it far?" She asks.

"No need to apologize. I find the way you talk fascinating." I smile down at her.

Avalon blushes slightly. I love the fact that my words make her color just so.

"We are going for a picnic. The place is not far from here. Do you mind walking or should I arrange for a carriage?" I ask her.

"Oh no, I can walk it. It will do me good to get some exercise. Popping in and out of places doesn't give me that." She replies.

I nod and offer her my arm. She politely accepts and places her small hand in the crook of my arm. I place my hand on top of hers and we walk toward the falls.

We walk through the meadow and come to the edge of the small river. Following the small river, we make our way to the pool from which the river is fed. We do not talk, and it does not seem that conversation is necessary. Underneath a large shade tree lies an enormous blanket laden with a basket, pillows and several towels. I smile.

I help Avalon down onto the blanket and support her with pillows for comfort before sitting down opposite her. Avalon leans over, opens the basket, peers inside and whistles low.

"What is it? Is there something wrong?" I ask quickly.

"No, nothing is wrong. You went all out, I see." She grins.

Confused, I look into the basket for myself. Two wine glasses complete with a skin of wine are surrounded by meats, cheeses, fruit and freshly baked bread. Small cakes are nestled between the wine glasses to cushion them.

"To be honest, the staff put this out. I just asked for a basket to be arranged for a picnic for us." I grin back at her and begin handing over items from the basket.

"Since you seem to know quite a bit about me, tell me about yourself." Avalon says before biting into a rather large strawberry.

"My mother sent me to Oonagh to be fostered here at court. Before that it was just my mother and I."

"What about your Dad?" She asks me.

"I do not know who my father is, my mother always avoids the question; after a while, I stopped asking." I reply.

"So, did you have any kind of father figure in your life?" Avalon prods.

"The only male figures I have been around is your grandfather." Avalon scoffs and I continue. "Also Oberon, Bain and Zephyr. If you are asking if I had anyone to teach me manly things, such as hunting, war-craft, strategy, and the like; I did not need a man for that, my mother is more than capable of teaching those." I answer her.

"Your mother sounds like a strong and interesting

woman. Does she come to see you often? I wouldn't mind meeting a woman like her." Avalon says.

"No, my mother has not come to see me since I arrived. I send her reports of my progress but that is all. Every once in a while I will get a message back from her but usually it is short and to the point." I explain. "If you would like to meet her, I can see if she will come out for a visit, or maybe we can go visit her." I offer.

Avalon shakes her head. "I can't leave right now. Things being what they are, my responsibilities, stuff I still need to learn, it makes leaving pretty much impossible. Maybe after everything has settled down?" She asks hopefully.

"Are you afraid to do anything now because of an old prophesy?" I challenge her.

"No, that isn't it. I have a decision to make. Once it is made, there isn't any way to go back. I feel like I'm carrying the weight of the world on my shoulders. I'm afraid that I will fail everyone." Avalon confesses.

"So you are not afraid for yourself, but for others you do not know?" I try to confirm.

"That is exactly it. What if I train to be this daughter of the Prophesy, and it turns out I'm a big flop? What if I accept my birthright and agree to be the Heir; then when the time comes to fulfill my duties, I let everyone down and the Sidhe goes into ruins?" She explains.

"That is what your friends are for, to be there for you when needed most. Someone to help with important decisions or talk through a dilemma you are having. You are not alone in any of this, Avalon. I am here for you. Oonagh, Oberon, Titania, Rob, Rion and many others are all here for you." I reach out trying to reassure her.

"What is troubling you about whatever decision that has to be made? If you care to talk about it, I will listen." I say quickly before she can say anything.

She sighs and I gesture for her to come closer. Avalon moves closer. I pull her gently over so that she is sitting in between my legs with her back facing my chest. I wrap my arms around her. She holds my arms there and breathes deep before resting her head back on my chest.

"I'm sorry for laying this all on you, it is nice to have someone to discuss my problems with." Avalon apologizes.

"You can lay anything you want on me. I am here for you, do not forget it." I gently admonish her.

Avalon giggles softly. "Okay, the thing is, I just found out the last piece of my genetic puzzle. If I go through with the Awakening, it may have an effect on my soul that wasn't intended."

I look down at her in confusion and sigh. "Quit talking in riddles. Please just tell me."

"I'm half Angel! Banished Angel! If I embrace that and go through the Awakening; when I die, I won't be allowed to go to heaven!" She exclaims and raises her face to look at mine. "You don't seem all that shocked at my revelation." Avalon states.

"I already knew you were half Angel. Do you think all children of the earth bound Angels are also banished from Heaven? Do you think that they have no salvation? I would like to think the children are not held accountable for the actions of their parents." I argue.

Avalon sighs. "I hope that what you say is true. Though if I embrace it to help save the world, I'd hope God would not hold that against me."

"If you truly believe that all Banished Angels have no salvation; you condemn me too." I say quietly, trying not to get upset. This a debate I have had with myself for decades.

Avalon looked at me, her eyes wide. "Oh, no." She shakes her head. "I didn't mean. I didn't know. I was just voicing my thoughts without thinking. I'm sorry."

I nod.

"Can I see them?" She asks softly.

"Are you hungry or could we hold off on eating until later?" I ask quickly taking off my shirt.

"I can eat later. What did you have in mind?" She asks curiously.

"A swim!" I grin and begin to pull down my pants.

Avalon turns around abruptly. "A bit of warning would have been nice!" She calls out with her back to me.

"Alright, but then you will not be able to see my wings." I say to her softly before jumping up and letting my wings explode forth, carrying me into the sky.

I look down and see Avalon turn at my words. She gets up and looks around, then starts to call my name. I love hearing the sound of my name on her lips. I dive down and plunge into the water below. The water is refreshing but not too cold. I break the surface of the water, shaking the water from my hair. Avalon stands there gazing at me, her skin a bit flush.

"Come join me, the water is nice!" I call out to her.

"I didn't bring a swimsuit!" She retorts.

"So? I did not bring one either." I laugh back, tucking my wings in closer to my body. "I will put them away if you do not come join me!" I tease her.

Avalon laughs. "Okay, fine." She jumps in with her sundress on.

Not quite what I had in mind but it is a step in the right direction. I smile.

CHAPTER 23

Avalon

I sit in my room thinking about the time I spent with Braelomdrel. We had a fun evening, and I have found a friend that might just be something more. If I allow it. The picnic and the swim was nice

Just one thing unnerved me about this evening. I mean what the hell was that? Just as I was about to have Braelomdrel turn around, there they were again. Those eyes. The feeling they invoked made me think better of stripping down to go into the water. A feeling of warmth passed over and chilled me a bit all at the same time.

I have never had a waking vision before. I tried playing it off so as to not let Braelomdrel know; I see things. The visions, I could do without him knowing about those. I do trust him, but there are just some things that should be secret. Not everyone should know everything about a person.

It is the third time I have seen those eyes. The first time, in my weird vision the first night here. The second, was during my training session with Aislinn. What is so important about those eyes? More importantly, who do they belong to?

I slip into bed with my thoughts in overdrive.

~*~

A tall figure stands in a clearing. From this distance, all I can tell is that the figure is male. His light brown hair is streaked with gold. His bronze skin has a glow to it that seems to be coming from within, not from the sun that lights the clearing. The figure he cuts is striking, well-muscled yet lean. His eyes seem to have a golden green glow to them. Maybe I'm imagining that part?

"I am pleased. You have been on my mind as much as I on yours." A deep soothing voice whispers to me.

Even though the man is quite a distance away, it feels as if he is speaking directly to my mind. Is this the form of communication all beings share after the Awakening?

"Who are you?" I call out.

"There is no need to shout out loud. I can hear you just fine. I am the other half of you." He says softly.

I gasp and my eyes widen. The clearing blurs and darkens. I sit up in my bed breathing heavily. There was no mistaking that vision. 'I am the other half of you' has only one meaning that I'm aware of. Someone that claims to be the other half of my soul that I have never met, I should be completely creeped out. Odd, I'm not creeped out by his revelation, just surprised. Most people are not that forward.

I lay back down trying to go back to sleep, hoping the man will come back so I can ask him more questions. Moments later, I am met with peaceful darkness.

CHAPTER 24

Nickolai

Teaching, training, sparring. That has been my life for the past month since we came back from the Sidhe. Well, I did make a trip out to my parents place to visit once. A visit to give my mom a reason for my absence that lasted over half a year. The story of meeting a girl and after the ordeal at work, I made sure she got to her family, but things just didn't work out between us. It was truth for the most part, I just had to leave out the extraordinary parts.

It seems so weird that the days I was in the Sidhe was actually months here. My inner beast loves to remind me daily that it is way past time to hunt. It is as if that side of me can actually feel the difference with the flow of time. It urges to come out more forcefully every day.

Today, I'm finally giving in. Rob is going to work with Drew and Melanie to teach the new Vampires, Sidhe techniques. I figured it would be best left to the expert to teach those. Now it is time to hunt, and let the beast within have his night.

I borrow Drew's Jeep and drive out of the area on Hwy 14, taking it all the way out to the Pawnee Grasslands. I park the Jeep at a small pullout parking lot that people use when they come hiking out here. At night, with the exception of the local wildlife, this place is deserted. I take off at a jog and then allow myself to shift. The beast comes roaring to life, literally.

I enjoy the primal run of my tiger form. The heightened senses. I lose myself to the run, the feel of the earth beneath my paws. My stomach growls and I instinctively take a whiff of the air.

I stop short. There is a smell in the air I haven't smelled before. It has a type of animal smell but there is something else that lies beneath. I sniff again. The smell is still there. It smells like another Were, but something still seems off. I crouch down low so that I'm below the high grass. I begin my hunt. Not to eat, but to investigate.

There, at the edge of the grasslands bordering on a line of trees, is my quarry. It is another Were-Tiger! Why does it smell different? I have not met another Were-Tiger but most Weres have a scent that distinguishes them as a Were. I watch closely from the tall grass. Ah ha! Well that explains the difference in smell, but how is she possible?

The female Were stops eating her kill. I notice the shift in the air. Crap, my cover is blown. The female bolts and I run after her. I need answers. She picks up speed and I do as well, trying to catch her. My muscles scream and burn. The thrill of the chase and answers I seek keep me moving.

A hard hit from the side sends me rolling in the tall grass. I stop and slowly pull myself upright and look around. Surrounding me are five Weres, all tigers! I sit down on my haunches and look at each Were in turn. I do not cower, but maintain my dominance.

The largest male walks right in front of me, sits down on his haunches and shifts. He looks right at me. I shift in return. I notice the rest shift as well. It seems as if I ran into a family. I was so focused on the female, that I didn't bother to sense for more. The middle aged man in front of me looks over at his wife that sits beside him. She nods at him and then looks over at her two teenage sons and her daughter. They look so much alike, it would be hard to mistake them for anything but family.

"I did not mean any harm." I spit out quickly. "I just have never seen another like me before; a female at that!"

The man stiffens. Oh crap. That didn't sound good to a father's ears, I'm sure.

"That isn't what I meant. I have never seen a female Were before, of any race. How is it possible? I was told it wasn't." I quickly backtrack.

The man relaxed a little. "How many are out here with you?" He asks.

"Just me." I blurt out and then wince. I just made myself very vulnerable.

The man nods. "You have shown your honesty with your

words which have left you vulnerable. I will extend the same courtesy. My name is Dimitri Volkov. This is my wife, Mila; my daughter, Katya; my sons, Viktor and Sergei."

I nod in return. Sergei seems familiar for some reason, but I can't place him. I don't bring it up and introduce myself instead, my questions already starting to bubble up inside me. "My name is Nickolai Savin. Do you live around here? Are there others?"

Dimitri looks at me a moment before answering. "We live further west, and there are others. A full community. If you are interested, you may join us. All those like us are welcome. Are there others where you are from?"

"Yes and no. Not tigers but wolves and other creatures." I say. "I would love the opportunity to visit and learn more about our shared culture."

Dimitri nods. Mila smiles warmly at me before looking at her children.

"You are welcome to visit any time young man. It is rare that we get to meet such a young man with some manners." Mila says before looking at her sons.

Katya snickers and Viktor shoots her a look. She shrugs. I notice Sergei remains quiet and doesn't respond to the obvious teasing. I wonder why but mention nothing of it.

"I would like that very much. Are you done hunting or can I join you? I did not mean to interrupt your hunt." I say.

"I would imagine if the tables were turned, I'd have done the same as you." Katya offers. "Come, let us go hunt together."

Katya shifts back and lopes off back towards her kill. The way Katya shifts seems to come naturally for her, as if she has been able to shift for a while. The others also shift and I join them. I notice they did not answer my question, but maybe they will tell me on my visit to the community. I'm curious how there are females. Rob said there weren't any, and that Avalon would not be able to shift. Clearly, he was wrong.

CHAPTER 25

Rob

I hear the crunch of gravel in front of the house as Nickolai abruptly parks my vehicle. The door bursts open and Nickolai rushes into the room. The look on Nickolai's face is one of excitement and something else I cannot quite place. Melanie and Drew come into the front room from the adjoining hallway to greet Nickolai.

"Brah, what is up with you? I haven't seen you like this since first meeting Avalon." Drew says after taking a quick glance at Nickolai.

My eyebrow raises. Could it be he has moved on from Avalon that quickly? Better for me if he has, for sure.

"You guys are not going to believe what I have discovered." Nickolai looks at me. "Especially you, something you've said before that wasn't possible!"

"Don't keep us all in suspense! What is it?" Melanie demanded with a laugh.

"Female Weres exist!" Nickolai shouts.

My head whips from Melanie to Nickolai with such intensity I feel like my neck just broke. "What?" I ask in disbelief.

"It's true! I met two of them tonight! I met a whole family of Weres that are just like me!" Nickolai says with joy.

I realize his happiness is not because he is over Avalon. It is because he has found others like himself. The implications of female Weres hit me. I need to find out how. If Avalon can also shift, this might be information she needs to know before the Awakening! By now, Avalon must have seen all the races she is made up of. It will be hard for her to concentrate if three forms are vying to push to the surface!

"Rob, are you okay?" Melanie asks.

"Yeah man, you just went whiter than Mel. I wouldn't have thought that possible until now." Drew quips.

"Are you going to see that family again?" I ask quickly.

"Yeah. Later today. Why, what is wrong?" Nickolai asks with concern.

"I need to know how the females exist." I choke out. "Avalon, knowing her as I do, she will go through the Awakening soon!" I feel sick.

"Man, you need to chill out a tad. You're turning green!" Drew says in worry as Melanie runs out of the room.

"I have Katya's number, I will see if they will give me the information over the phone." Nickolai replies and walks back out of the front door while dialing her number.

"Hurry, I will need to warn her quickly." I croak out.

Melanie comes back to the room and hands me a glass of water. I try to calm down and sip the water slowly.

After what seems like hours, even though it was only fifteen minutes, Nickolai walks back into the front room. I look at him expectantly.

"According to Dimitri, his wife and daughter can only shift because Sergei had a vial of water with him when he took the opportunity to escape from Morcant last September. There is a healer in their community that is a descendant from the original shaman of our clan." Nickolai says and I look at him oddly at the last part. "Dimitri found my family line, the community thought we were wiped out. Anyway, the only reason his daughter and wife could shift is because the same mixture was used to originally create us in the first place. I think without the mix of the water and the panther blood, Avalon will not shift." Nickolai continues.

I let out a short sigh of relief, but then another thought comes to mind.

"Nickolai, what is to stop them from making more Weres?" I ask him.

"The water supply. It is gone. The damage has been done. The whole community can shift except for children under 5." Nickolai replies.

"How did there come to be so many in one community? How did they know to gather?" I push for more information.

"I don't know. I can find out during my visit." Nickolai offers.

"That will be good. For now, learn what you can. See if they would be willing to join us. I need to get back to the Sidhe and advise the council of this new information." I inform him.

I look to Nickolai, Drew and Melanie. "I need the three of you to head things here. Keep up with the training, all of you are well skilled in the fighting styles of the Sidhe, make sure the others are as well. I will be back in touch with you soon." I advise them before leaving the house. I run as fast as my muscles will allow. I must get to the closest ley-line quickly. I just hope the rest are ready for this new development and its potential ups and downs.

~*~

I walk through the gateway and step out into the courtyard. Bain stands nearby and closes the gateway behind me. I walk off towards the Great Hall, hoping to catch the King or Queen in order to call a council meeting. The double doors to the Great Hall open before me; I am in luck. Finvarra and Oonagh are both present. I present myself to Finvarra before advising we need to hold a quick impromptu council meeting.

Avalon and Braelomdrel walk into the Great Hall, looking quite close. I can feel my jealousy rise up. Not everything is as it seems, I chide myself, besides there are more pressing matters. Soon the Great Hall is filled with only council members.

"Your Majesties, fellow council members. I must share with you a new development in our cause. This new development can have some consequences that will have to be looked into further at a later time. Nickolai, friend to the Sidhe, has uncovered a full community of Were-Tigers! This community includes shifting females, in fact, everyone over the age of five can shift." I announce to the Council.

Several audible gasps fill the room. "*How?*" The question echoes in my mind as most of the council members ask the same thing at once. I cover my ears in gesture, the voices in my mind are deafening. As quickly as it started, the noise subsides.

"Our apologies." Oonagh says as she looks around the room. Almost every person has flushed faces.

"Accepted. To answer your question, I only know just a bit of the basics. My first inquiry was for the safety of our Princess." I nod to Avalon. The noise picks up again but in concern for Avalon. Avalon smiles at me and mouths words of thanks. I smile back.

"From what I learned, should the Princess chose to go through the Awakening, she need not be worried about a third form trying to come to the surface. She should not be able to shift. The women of the community were given a mixture similar to what we gave the males centuries ago."

"What is to stop them from making more?" A voice rose up.

"Water supply, I hope." I reply.

"With the females now with active Were genes, will it spread to their offspring; boys and girls alike?" Another voice calls out.

"I do not know. As I said before, the actions of this community may have some consequences that we may need to discuss later once we know more. For now, Nickolai is going to try convincing them into joining us. It is a possibility we will have a much larger force than expected on Earth."

I look around to see that everyone is happy with the news of a stronger force. It is time I let them in on the rest of the secret.

"On matters of our force, I need to let you all know of another development. When I went back with Nickolai, we found more than expected. Melanie, a Vampire, brought many more back to Carl's home when she returned from the fight with Morcant."

"Abominations!" Finvarra shouts.

"Yes, however, they are behind us to the death. They want revenge against Morcant for the lives they must lead now. These men and women were changed without their knowledge. I would like to task our greatest minds to see if there is a way to reverse what was done to them. If there is a way found, we can reverse the effects after the defeat of Morcant." I argue.

There is a murmur of agreement around the room.

Avalon stands up abruptly. "As Heir, I claim these men

and women, who were forcibly changed, under my protection. No one is to act against them. If anyone goes against this, I will see to it they are punished within the fullest extent of Sidhe law." She states loudly.

I look around the room. Most council members seem to be in agreement with her. Oonagh and Braelomdrel are positively beaming at her. Did she just declare her choice, however vaguely? I look to Finvarra. The jaw muscles on his face working vigorously. I have to give Avalon credit, she has learned how to make a preemptive strike against her grandfather. I could not be more proud of the woman she is becoming.

CHAPTER 26

Avalon

I don't exactly know when I'd made my decision. It was out there now, everyone heard my declaration. I had a feeling that if it wasn't spoken, my grandfather might have done something about the abominations. I really had made my decision after the night with Braelomdrel. His argument made sense. Why would God extend the punishment of the Banished Angels to their offspring? If he intends to, then my sacrifice for all these people is worth it. If I can help these people, even if it leads to my death, it is worth it.

I look around and notice only a few understand the meaning in my words. Grandmother, Braelomdrel, Rob and Grandfather; only the first three seem to be pleased. I think my grandfather was secretly hoping I'd decline. What is he so afraid of? I'm not about to kill him to take his throne, he must know this. Right?

I catch my grandmother looking at me intently. I don't

know what she wants. I look back at her in slight confusion. She looks to Braelomdrel, who nods.

"Your grandmother would like you to formally announce it." Braelomdrel leans down and whispers in my ear.

"Oh." I breathe out.

I look back to my grandmother and acknowledge her request.

"I have decided to go through the Awakening and formally take my place as Heir. The ceremony will commence at sunset." I announce to the room.

A chorus of blessings and astounding approval fills the room. I smile as my stomach begins to turn in nervous, anxious knots.

~*~

It is official. I need a full bucket of Tums! Nervous anxiety has completely taken over! Amberley has tried to calm my nerves by talking about everything but what I'm about to do. She did make me look absolutely gorgeous! My miracle worker, I must confess. The loose semi-transparent blue gown she has me in is belted at my waist with a silver cord. There are even hidden slits in the back so that my dress isn't torn to shreds when my wings eventually explode out of my back. Just the thought makes me cringe.

"Are you sure people won't see through this?" I ask Amberley for the millionth time.

"No one will be trying to see you naked. They will be

more concerned that you come out of this alive. Though I am proud of your decision, it worries me. Your brother has not chosen to do this, for the very reasons of my worry. His will ultimately be worse, if he does. Three races battling the fourth for control." Her face looks terrified at the prospect.

"That isn't helping." I admonish Amberley.

"Sorry Princess. I worry, but you will do fine. I am sure." Amberley says reassuringly.

I hear a soft rap against the outer door of my suite. Amberley answers the door and allows Rion entry.

"Ready for this?" Rion asks.

"As ready as I'll ever be." I reply in resignation.

"You don't have to do this." Rion states.

"Yes, I do." I affirm.

"As long as you are sure. I don't want you feeling pressured to do this." Rion acknowledges.

"There is always going to be some pressure, but I do this of my own choosing. Our people need us, even if we didn't know they existed not long ago." I tell him.

Rion nods but says nothing more. He offers up his arm and I take it. We walk out of my suite and toward whatever the future decides to bestow on us.

~*~

A large bonfire marks the center of the circle. It feels as if everyone in the Sidhe is here; it's so crowded! There are several smaller fires lit along the outside edge of the gathering. The air feels as if it is charged with energy. Fireflies light the way to the circle as Rion escorts me. The butterflies in my stomach seem to have gotten loose, I'm so nervous!

We reach the center of the circle and there are two robed figures I haven't met yet. Beside the robed figures stand my grandparents and Braelomdrel. Rion releases my hand and stands in between our grandmother and Braelomdrel. The gathering quiets down until there is nothing but eerie silence. Even the nocturnal animals and bugs are silent.

"Avalon, Daughter of Trieva, Granddaughter of King Finvarra and Queen Oonagh, Heir to the High Throne; do you enter this ceremony of your own choosing?" A deep voice intones from one of the robed figures.

"I do." I reply.

"Do you accept the responsibilities and the consequences this choice may bring?" A robed figure asks.

"I do." I answer again.

"May you be blessed. May you live." A robed figure states.

The second robed figure pours the bright blue liquid from an extremely old fashioned water-skin into a small cup. The figure then stands directly in front of me and brings the cup up to my lips. The hand holding the cup seems familiar.

"Drink and be Awakened. Drink and become one with the Sidhe." The man in the robe says and tips the cup against my lips pouring its contents into my mouth.

I swallow the liquid and wait for something to happen. I look around searching the faces around me for clues of what is to come. It hits me. The wave of fire rushing through me. Every part of me hurts. I can feel parts of my body changing on their own. I try to think about what Amberley said before. I can't think it hurts too much!

"You can do this, you will come out of this alive and well. Think of the form your mother's family has, it is not much different. Focus on that form." A soothing voice says softly but sternly, the voice seems to dampen the pain.

I know no one is close enough to speak to me like that. I recognize the voice. It is the one from my dream. From the one that claims he is the other part of me. Who is he? I want to hear him again, if only to relieve the pain!

"Stay focused. I will always be here for you through this link. I may not be able to see or touch you but by your side is where I belong." He says again.

"I'm so tired. I just want it to stop! It feels like it will never end!" I cry out to the voice.

Pain rips through my back. My body feels as if it is being lifted. My body hits the ground hard, any breath that I had left escapes. The pain subsides and the darkness envelops me.

CHAPTER 27

Braelomdrel

I know we are just supposed to witness Avalon's Awakening but this is hard. No one here has had to go through the strain her body is going through. Her body fluctuates between skin and scale. I can see the buds of her wings wanting to spring forth. Every time they get close, her body shifts again. All I want to do is take her in my arms. To comfort her and ease this transition.

Her body stops shifting into scales finally and is covered in skin once more. Her wings spring forth from the skin and she raises up. Wings gloriously spread, she is quite a sight to behold. Her dark hair slowly changes to a blinding white. The look her eyes hold, seem to be of blindness, but the color has changed in them too. Does she know what is going on or is pain all she feels? Suddenly, Avalon's body plummets back to the ground. She lands hard on her back. Her head hits the ground.

We are supposed to wait until the Awakened have completed their transition to approach. I can no longer stand by and watch. I do not care that this will show my weakness or vulnerability. Over the past two weeks this girl has shown a fire within her that cannot be subdued yet is willing to show me her vulnerabilities. This girl is mine and I will do everything possible to protect her!

I move from my position within the Ceremony and walk to Avalon's side. I can hear the mutterings from the gathering. I do not care what they think! I move my hands under Avalon, picking her up slowly and gently. I gaze around the gathered while holding Avalon in my arms. The look on Oonagh's face is one of amusement and surprise, her eyes wide and lips tucked inward as if she is trying to stop herself from smiling.

Avalon stirs in my arms and I look down at her face. She is looking up at me in confusion.

"Brae?" Avalon asks and then closes her eyes tight.

I bring her closer to my face and lower my head. "Are you okay Avalon? Should I put you down?" I ask softly.

"What happened? My body feels like I've been hit by a truck." She groans slightly.

"For a while I was not sure which form you would take. Your body kept shifting between what you are and a Merrow. Then it seemed as if you finally focused on one and your wings sprouted. Unfortunately, your wings lifted you up and when your body shifted back to wingless, you fell. Hard." I explain, feeling the eyes of the gathered on me.

"I thought no one was supposed to touch me during this. Why are you carrying me?" She asks, looking around at the crowd.

"After you fell, I could not take it. I could not stand to see you hurting without providing comfort." I say while slowly lowering her back to the ground.

I steady her as she gains stability.

"I am sorry. I upset you." I say quickly.

"No, you didn't. I was just surprised to see you. You broke ceremonial formalities for my well-being. I'm not at all upset with you." She assures me.

She walks toward her family and shows the gathered that she is complete and whole. The gathering closes in for closer inspection and cheers. Those closest to Avalon, one at a time, begin to take her hand in theirs and whisper what sounds to be a simple blessing. The gathering then makes their way to the Great Hall.

I enter the Great Hall, it is packed. There is barely any room to move. Finvarra, Oonagh, Avalon and Rion ascend to the top of the dais. Now was the moment of truth. Would the stone sing for her?

Finvarra looks at Avalon a moment and she winces slightly. Finvarra was either too forceful in his mind-speak or Avalon is still too sensitive. He then gestures for her to walk over and touch the pillar on the far side of the dais. She walks gingerly across the dais. Avalon tentatively stretches out her arm and stops, noticing briefly the color of her hair for the first time. The look of surprise is on her face but for a moment before she continues toward the pillar. Just as her fingertips graze the pillar, a loud, clear, piercing tone fills the room. I smile broadly. The stone sings for her!

I glance back at Finvarra, his jaw twitches slightly in annoyance. Finvarra quickly plasters a big smile on his face. Putting on a show, no doubt. Avalon will see right through that. I watch Avalon, she is smiling back at Finvarra and the rest of her family. She then turns to the gathered masses and beams brightly.

~*~

I lay on my bed, stretched out and ready for sleep. The evening is warm even with the breeze coming through the windows.

"You better not be asleep." The voice of my mother comes from the bowl on the other side of my room.

I sigh loudly. "Well I am definitely not now." I call out.

I get up off the bed and trudge over to the bowl sitting on the table. I look down into the bowl and see my mother looking back at me.

"How did it go? Did she go through with it?" My mother asks impatiently.

"She did. I was afraid for her for a while. Her body kept shifting back and forth between forms. I am not surprised she passed out at the end. Though the fall could have knocked her out." I reply.

"Fall?" My mother prods me, a look of concern on her face.

"Her wings sprouted and lifted her in the air, then her body shifted again and she fell to the ground. She is okay now." I say and shift my stance.

Eyes narrowed, my mother looks at me sternly for a moment before speaking. "What did you do? I can see it in your body language, you did something. Out with it!" She demands.

"I could not watch her be hurt. No one else here has had to go through a transition like that before. No one was allowed to walk her through it! After she fell I went to her and picked her up. I was carrying her when she woke." I explain.

"I have always drilled it into you to never show weakness. Here you are, displaying it blatantly for the whole community. I can see the change in you. You love the girl. Am I correct?" My mother admonishes me.

"I like her very much. I ..." I manage to get out before stopping myself.

"I see, you have not come to the realization yourself yet." My mother chuckles. "What was her reaction to what you did? Was she happy to see you? Was she mad that you ruined her ceremony?" My mother quickly fires questions at me.

"At first she was surprised to see me. I do not know if she was expecting someone else or just surprised someone was holding her. She was not angry with me. She seemed pleased that I had broken formality." I respond quickly.

"Good, she may not know her feelings for you herself. Keep nurturing this friendship you have, it should blossom nicely." My mother croons.

"What about the Stone?" My mother asks in almost an afterthought.

"It sang. Loudly. The sound started to hurt my ears." I cringe.

"Ha!" My mother claps her hands together in glee and notices the look on my face. "Oh, I am not glad that the Stone hurt your ears. The Stone barely made a tone at all when Finvarra touched it. The fact that it made any sound at all was enough for the Dagda I suppose." She explains.

I nod. "Will that be all?"

"You have done well my son. With the exception of your faux pas, but if she does not hold it against you, then who am I to judge." My mother smiles and her image fades from the water.

CHAPTER 28

Avalon

I keep thinking about the large stone pillar from last night. It even consumed my dreams. Not the pillar, but something inside of it. That sounds totally crazy, maybe it is just side effects from what happened last night. I can't believe my first exposure to mind-speak was with Finvarra. He would have been one of my last choices. Something about that last thought seemed off to me, a nagging feeling, like I'm missing something.

"Good morning Princess. Are you feeling up to breakfast this morning?" Amberley asks gently while setting a tray down on the small table.

My stomach growls loudly and Amberley laughs.

"I take that as a yes. I was not sure you would be ready for food yet with your ordeal last evening." Amberley confesses. "Luckily I brought you something from the kitchen, just in case."

"Thank you for taking such good care of me Amberley. I don't know what I'd do without you." I say, rising out of bed.

I sit down to a plate of eggs, bacon and pancakes. Unable to wait any longer, I dig into the plate of food. I don't know that I've ever been this hungry before.

"Amberley?" I call out to get her attention.

"Yes Princess?" Amberley says, poking her head out from my bathroom.

"Can you help me work on this mindspeak thing? I don't want to react to contact like last night with my grandfather. It is natural for others to talk that way, right?"

"Some prefer that method of communicating. I will certainly help you get used to it. In time, you will be able to put up a block so that not just anyone can enter your mind. Most are considerate and wait for you to allow them in. What your grandfather did last night was rude, to say the least." Amberley states firmly.

"So how does this mind-speak thing work? How can I do it too?" I ask her.

"For beginners, we always teach them to make eye contact with who they want to speak with. Once you get used to doing this and are familiar with the technique, looking someone in the eyes is not necessary. You must focus what you want to say along with meanings behind it. Some of us will see the images in your mind as you talk. It is not always what you say but what is being thought of at the time. Be conscious of that." Amberley replies.

I look at Amberley intently. *"Amberley?"* I think at her.

"I can hear you my dear. You are doing extremely well for your first try." Amberley smiles at me.

"I have something that has been bugging me lately. Do many people like my grandfather? Sometimes I think they don't. I wouldn't blame them either."

"Most of us put up with him because we have no other choice. His power affects most of us and we bend to his will. That is why so many of us are happy that you are here. Our future looks brighter with you in it."

I nod. *"I had dreams about the stone last night. More importantly something inside it. It feels so weird, but I've had the oddest sensation to go back to it since I woke."*

Amberley's eyes widen. *"What exactly have you seen in your dreams? I have heard of your dreams before, most of us have. The word of your gifts have spread among the people."*

"The stone seems to glow blue from within. The blue light pulses and gets brighter as I approach it. The brightness of the glow is concentrated in a small spot near the top of the stone, like there is something inside it. That something is what is glowing, not the stone itself." I try to explain, showing her the images from my dream.

Amberley's mouth pops open slightly in surprise. *"I wondered where it went. When it was removed from the standing stone in Ireland many centuries ago for safe keeping, no one knew where the treasure was put."*

My ears perk up. *"Treasure? Amberley what are you talking about?"*

"No one has told you of the four treasures of the Sidhe? They are all part of the Prophesy. I guess they decided not to speak of it until you made your decision. The object taken from the standing stone is the Lia Fáil, also known as the Stone of Truth. It is one of the treasures brought to the Sidhe when the original members of the Tuatha de Danann arrived in Ireland."

"How do you know all this Amberley? You describe it as if you were there."

"I was, but that is a tale for another time. It is more important that you know what I am about to share."

I nod. This woman is definitely older than she looks. I can table her tale for later. I really want to know more.

"The other three treasures are the Cauldron of Dagda, the Spear of Lug and the Sword of Nuada."

My eyes widen in surprise. Rob talked about the Cauldron. *"I have heard of the Cauldron."* I interrupt Amberley and she looks at me curiously.

"How?"

"Rob mentioned it to us back in Colorado. He never mentioned the others though. Rob said that Morcant must have it since he is able to sort of awaken people."

Amberley nods. *"That makes sense. It would also seem that our friends had the gift of foresight like you."*

"What friends?" I look back at Amberley in confusion.

184

"*The friends that made your necklace. With the last of their great magic they created a failsafe. Your necklace is not just what it appears to be. It is a key. The Cauldron can only be controlled by a male, the key allows the bearer to be able to control the Cauldron in time of great need. A piece of the other three treasures will fit inside of your necklace, enabling it to become the key.*"

"*Where are these friends now? Did they die after using their gifts for us?*"

"*They have not been seen since we were presented with this last gift. I do not know what has happened to them.*"

"*I think a visit to the stone is needed. Would you like to join me?*"

"*I think your visit should be made after a shower and fresh clothes.*" Amberley giggles.

~*~

Amberley and I enter the Great Hall finding it deserted. I make my way up to the pillar with Amberley at my side. The pillar begins to glow a faint blue as I approach. I wonder if it did this last night. I never noticed it. I touch the pillar again and the tone rings out again. Then I notice an opening towards the back of the pillar that faces away from the rest of the room. I look into it and see a small bright blue stone glowing inside.

I remove the stone from the pillar and feel an odd sensation of something moving underneath my shirt. I open the neck of my shirt and watch in awe as the dragon on the necklace moves. I carefully bring the pendant out of my shirt and a claw is extended, as if reaching for the stone.

"Give the dragon the stone Avalon." Amberley nudges me.

I nod and carefully give the stone to the dragon. The claw closes around the stone and brings it back into the pendant. The dragon stops moving but now it looks like the stone has always been there.

"What are you doing in here?" My grandfather demands.

"I am retrieving the stone for what needs to be done next." I state.

"What stone? That stone doesn't move. The stone is where it belongs." My grandfather says irritably.

I turn around with the pendant still outside of my shirt. "Too late. The stone is under new management."

"So you think you have figured out the prophesy? You think that is part of it? How did you get that stone in the pendant?" My grandfather fires quickly.

"That prophesy doesn't make a whole lick of sense to me. The visions I have had, the fact that it glows for me, and that the dragon took the stone into the pendant means it's where it belongs for now." I reply coolly.

My grandfather raises an eyebrow.

"To be perfectly honest, I don't know what your problem is with me. I'm your granddaughter and legitimate heir. I have no clue why you insist on treating me as someone barely above dirt. I'm not here to take away your throne but to succeed you, if that is what you're afraid of." I fire at him before he can get a word out.

My grandfather looks stunned for a moment. Could it be that he didn't know how his actions and speech came off to people? A small part of me wants to believe that is the case; that he doesn't hate me.

"My dear, I apologize if that is how my mannerisms have affected you. You are my granddaughter and heir, not my only heir; I need to get used to you and your mannerisms as well." My grandfather admits with some tactful grace.

"*I do not fear you taking my thrown.*" My grandfather mind-speaks to me.

Though I hear his words, the thoughts swirling inside him say different. He has seen how the people have taken to me. He is afraid of something. Whatever he is afraid of is quickly veiled from me and I can't see it. Whatever it is, the form I saw along with that feeling of fear was a man.

"*Then we should have no problems.*" I reply back with a smile.

"Since I now have part of the key, the next stage of my path has begun. I need to know about the next treasure and where to start looking to find it." I state quickly. "The sooner these pieces are found; the sooner this whole mess is sorted."

My grandfather smiles in approval. "The next treasure is the Sword of Lug, which should be the easier of the two to obtain until your abilities fully mature. No one in the Sidhe knows its location, however, I do know of one that may be of assistance to find the sword. Seek out Deverril. He can be found at the well whose waters run red."

Really? No clue other than a well with red water,

seriously? Since this has been the most cordial conversation I've ever had, I say nothing as to what I really think of his help. He did give me a name, and that is something. I nod.

"I shall take a group with me to seek out and secure our treasure. We will bring it back to where it belongs." I say solemnly and bow my head slightly in respect.

"Send word to Rob and Braelomdrel that I need to speak with them at once." I advise Amberley who nods in acknowledgment.

~*~

I sit in my room, fingering the dragon pendant and the shiny, blue stone. I have no idea how we will find a certain sword that is hidden somewhere on Earth. A couple realizations dawn on me. First, I can't ever go back to Earth to live. The Sidhe is my home now, where I belong. Secondly, Earth seems more like it's a different planet or plane than the one I live on. I wonder how that could be.

I feel a sharp spark in my fingertip and my room fades from view. The space that surrounds me looks similar to the blue of the stone. Slowly two images start to fade into view. Two faces, profiles of men, their face shapes are similar. My grandfather is on the left. Who is that on the right? He looks familiar. The faces rotate towards me and I gasp. Morcant! Why am I seeing this? I step closer to both faces and notice similarities, too many of them. They are related! How?

The images before me start to shift again, a hand touches my shoulder and the vision fades. I look up and see Amberley looking at me with concern in her eyes. Behind her is Rob and Braelomdrel. Crap! I didn't want him to know about this!

CHAPTER 29

Melanie

Nickolai walks in through the door after another visit with Katya. They have been meeting each other several times over the last month.

"When do we get to meet Katya?" I ask Nickolai.

"She will be here later this evening for a visit. I had a feeling the two of you would be chomping at the bit to meet her." Nickolai says quickly.

"Oh! Does she know about the house situation?" I say hesitantly.

"No, Dimitri would not have let her come if he knew we had a house full of Vampires. It wouldn't matter if they were in control of themselves or not." Nickolai laughs. "Don't worry. I will explain to her once she gets here."

"It isn't like we would want to eat her." I retort.

"That isn't quite what I meant. New Vampires tend to get out of hand combatively before they have really learned control. New Weres are the same. They just tend to go after each other. If Sergei told his family about the Vampires, they would be on guard." Nickolai informs us.

"Sergei Volkov? He is alive?" Drew asks in surprise.

"You know him?" Nickolai asks.

"Yeah, I wasn't sure if Katya and Dimitri were the same ones I knew. Sergei and I used to run in the same groups for 4H. I know the whole family. I just didn't know about the community. He was on the crew that should have come to help aid us at work." Drew explains, his voice trails off on the last part.

"Ah. Now I know why he looked familiar. It would explain how he came to have a vial of the water as well. There is much we don't know yet." Nickolai muses.

~*~

I hear the others playing in the new game room we set up downstairs after Nickolai came back. It has brightened their spirits a bit as half of them seemed to be wallowing in mourning of the lives they once had. Everyone is having some fun again and it is nice to hear laughter.

A rap on the door ends the laughter and playfulness. I can feel the entire house on edge. The ones below are silent, waiting to see what is going on. I hear Nickolai walk to the front door and open it. Giving them space, I sit waiting with Drew on the couch. I hear the sharp intake of breath.

Nickolai just told her. I fidget, trying to wait patiently. Drew grabs my hand and squeezes reassuringly.

I hear footsteps come through the doorway from the front room and into the open living area. I turn slowly, trying not to startle Katya. Her heart is beating so fast. Her fear is permeating the air.

"There is no need to be afraid of us. We want to meet you. We want to become friends." I say softly, trying not to sound creepy.

"Katya!" Drew calls out and rises from the couch.

Almost immediately the fear leaves Katya. She recognizes Drew.

"Drew?" Katya looks dumbfounded.

"You will be safe here. Don't worry!" Drew motions to me. "Katya, this is my girl, Melanie. I assure you we are all friends here."

The last bit of tension seems to ease off of Katya's body and she nods.

"It's nice to meet you. I apologize if I've made you feel uncomfortable in your own home." Katya says softly.

"It's nice to meet you too. Don't worry, I've been uncomfortable since my change." I laugh slightly. "This is a friend's house, she is letting us use it due to our circumstances. Make yourself comfortable." I smile at her.

Katya smiles back and sits next to Nickolai on the love seat.

"The others are downstairs. We decided not to overwhelm you. You will hear the noise go back up once they are sure everything is alright." I chuckle as the music and the voices grow louder from the basement below. "See?"

Katya nods in thanks still smiling.

"I can't help but staring. Sergei's description of Vampires were much different." Katya apologizes.

"He was used to helping us round up new Vampires. Melanie and the others are still considered new by most standards but they are in control of themselves, unlike the ones your brother was used to." Nickolai explains. "Melanie is actually the fastest one to adapt to the change that I have ever seen."

"I'm not sure if I should take that as a compliment or not." I say giving Nickolai a funny look.

"Don't screw your face up like that. It might get stuck that way." Drew quips.

Katya, Nickolai and I laugh.

"It was meant as a compliment. I know you don't enjoy being a Vampire, but your ability to adapt so quickly amazes me." Nickolai replies.

"How did you change? Why are there so many of you here? Nickolai didn't explain that." Katya said.

"She and the others were changed around the same time that Sergei came back to your family. The man that took Sergei, had a mass recruitment scheduled here in Colorado.

Melanie and the ones downstairs were the result of it. Well part of it. We haven't found any of the people that changed into other beings yet." Drew explains.

Katya smiles. "I think we can help each other then. Our community grew as well 10 months ago. There are more than just Were-Tigers there. Sergei told Dad about what happened. We were able to get those that came out of the building after it happened."

My eyes widen. I look to Drew and Nickolai, who are wearing the same expression.

"How many came to join your community?" I ask her.

"Over forty. They don't exactly live in our area but they come out for meetings and social gatherings. There are some people in the community, I didn't know their kind existed!" Katya explains. "Are there others like that here?"

"There used to be. Some come in for a time and then leave again. The one that owns this house is that way, so is her twin brother." Nickolai replies.

"Katya, would your father and the community be willing to join us and others in a fight against Morcant? To stop him and his followers from wreaking havoc on our world and beyond?" Drew asks.

"Beyond? You piqued my curiosity now Drew. As to joining you, I'd imagine the community would be willing, it is a topic best brought to a gathering. There is one tomorrow. If you will excuse me a moment, I will go call my father. I need to get permission to extend an invitation to all three of you."

Katya says as she stands up and plucks a phone from her back pocket.

"Sure." We say in unison.

"Jinx. You both owe me a Coke!" Drew yells out.

We all laugh.

"There's the laugh I like to hear." Drew grins at me.

"Why thank you, I didn't know you liked my laugh so much." Nickolai quips.

I laugh again and the guys grin.

"Nickolai, have you heard anything from Rob about Avalon and her Awakening?" I ask tentatively.

"No. I'm hoping no news, is good news. I overheard many things while there. Things I don't think they thought I'd hear. Apparently, Avalon has the blood of four different races flowing through her. We know about the Merrow, Human and Were-Panther from Carl. However, I wasn't able to find out what the ruling family is."

"FOUR?" I choke out. "Carl was a mess with the Merrow and the Were fighting his human side. I thought mine was bad. I feel so sorry for her." I say in worry.

"Okay." Katya walks back into the room, not realizing she interrupted. "I can extend an offer for the three of you to join us at the gathering in a few days. Dinner and festivities are included. It will be a time of information sharing and then you can make your proposal." Katya grins at us.

~*~

The music is pumping loudly as we pull up to the large farm. Nickolai looks to be at ease with all this, but I'm nervous as all get out. I clench and unclench my hands trying to squeeze out the nerves. I don't think I've ever been around this many Weres in my short existence as a Vampire, not even at the mines. I will be the only Vampire here. I know Nickolai and Drew won't let anything happen to me, but there are so many more Weres and their attitudes towards my kind that it is hard to know how they will all react.

"Relax." Drew rubs my arms and back after I get out of the Jeep. "You're radiating nervousness. Be the confident, chick I know you to be. You've got this babe."

I smile back at him. He always seems to know exactly how I'm feeling and what I need to hear. I push my nerves and doubt deep down and look back at Drew, who nods.

"Let's do this." I smile at Drew and he grins back; the dimple on his cheek peeking back at me.

Drew takes my hand in his. We walk toward the gathering where Nickolai and Katya wait. Katy Perry's Firework song, blares out of the sound system and I can't help but bounce a little to the beat. The throng envelops us once we reach Nickolai and Katya. I look around and most are around our age. The older people are off to the sides with young kids or yammering away like my grandparents used to do.

Katya guides us through the throng to an older gentleman who is surrounded by men and women. I can feel their stares on me without even looking directly at them. I keep my eyes on the older gentleman, his looks are similar to Katya's. Possibly her dad?

"Welcome!" Dimitri calls out with a smile on his face. "The fact that you accepted my invitation and braved the den of Weres tells me a great deal, young lady." Dimitri smiles at me.

"Thank you. I was a ball of nerves before arriving here, I'll admit." I reply.

"You are nothing like what my Sergei told me of Vampires." Dimitri muses.

"To be honest, Dimitri, Sergei was only used to brand new Vampires; the variety that have no self-control. Melanie, has exceptional control." Drew interjects but omits to mention the others at the house.

"I see. Are there others like you?" Dimitri asks me directly.

"Not quite like me, but there are others. They all have full self-control. Please do not worry. Not one of us wish any harm to your community." I reply quickly.

Dimitri nods. "I'm curious to learn more, but it will have to be at a later time. The three of you will come to the council gathering of elders later tonight. We will discuss matters then." Dimitri dismisses us as food is brought out and dinner begins.

~*~

I sit with Drew at the bonfire, where the others of our

age are gathered. I feel a slight tap on my left shoulder and look up. Dimitri motions for us to follow. I get up and follow Dimitri, with Drew, Nickolai and Katya trailing behind me. Dimitri ushers us into a large barn. The inside looks more like a gathering hall. The floor is made of wood and not strewn with hay and dirt from animals. A slight animal scent lingers in the air. At this point, I'm not sure if it is from animals or the amount of Weres congregated in a confined space. Large hanging chandeliers made of antlers light the room.

I'd half expected some of the people here to show their distaste for my presence. I didn't see that on any of the faces gathered; more curiosity than anything. I sat toward the front as directed with Drew and Nickolai. Katya sat down in a chair near the wall with some other people our age.

"Welcome friends and guests." Dimitri calls out in opening. "Tonight, we will be learning more about our newest friends here. Apparently we have a common enemy."

Eyes widen around the room. Hushed tones of murmurs flood the room.

"Sergei shared his story with us last year and brought a transformation to our group. Drew, please introduce your friends to the group. I'm sure you have already noticed familiar faces here." Dimitri motions for us to stand up and face the people in the room.

"Hey all." Drew greets everyone with a wave of his hand. "Nickolai is the serious one over here, and this is Melanie." Drew gestures to the two of us.

"All three of us were changed because of Morcant.

Although Nickolai and I agreed to the change, just like Sergei, Melanie didn't. Melanie and those like her, were given no choice. It was a forced change. I'm sure you all know what Melanie is, it's not hard to tell she isn't a Were or Fae like us."

"Aren't all Vampires minions of Morcant?" A voice calls out.

"Most, except for her and twenty four others. All of them were changed against their will. All of them want to see the end of Morcant and his followers. They want to stop them just as much as we do, so that this can't be done to anyone else." Drew explains.

Multiple heads nod in agreement.

"Nickolai has more information to share that he's witnessed firsthand." Drew announces, takes my hand and leads me back to the chairs.

We sit down as Nickolai nervously clears his throat.

"What I'm about to share with you all, I only learned of right after the incident here in Colorado. First off, are there any stories amongst the community on how Weres came about?" Nickolai asks the group.

"An old tale has always been that we were once guardians of some gate." An old man's voice croaked out.

"Our races came about from magic, our ancestors were changed by this. Our forms come from the animal our ancestors thought were the fiercest. The gates they guarded were the entrances into the Sidhe." Nickolai fills in the gaps to the old man's brief explanation.

"The Sidhe! An old wives tale!" The same man croaked out again.

"Is it? Our races were formed from the water held sacred by the Sidhe and the blood of the animal the ancestors chose. I would bet that is how your women are now able to shift." Nickolai fires back.

Audible gasps and stunned faces fill the gathered group. Good one Nick!

"That is exactly how we were able to let our females change. We tried it on a whim. Kari, here, works for the Denver Zoo and was able to procure the blood samples we needed. How exactly do you now all this, son?" Dimitri asks curiously.

"I know the Heir to the High Throne of the Sidhe. One of her top protectors was who informed me almost a year ago. The Sidhe really does exist and I have been there. The group here and ours aren't alone in the fight against Morcant. We have the full backing of the Sidhe and they will aid us." Nickolai explains.

"Do you have any proof of this other than your word?" Dimitri cautiously asks.

"Ladies and Gentlemen," Drew starts. "I was there when Nickolai appeared with two men in our living room bringing the good news less than a week ago."

"What do you mean, appeared? I thought they used gateways?" Dimitri inquires in alarm.

"Apparently, they don't always need to use them. I'm not

versed on how it all works." Nickolai states. "However, you have nothing to fear from them either. Our friend, her father would have been one with this community had he survived during our run-in with Morcant. He was a Were-Panther. She carries the Were-gene."

"Then how is she the Heir to the High Throne?" Mila probes.

"Through her mother's side. I have met them, the family she has left, and they are all backing this." Nickolai says firmly.

"Have they stated when they want to strike?" Dimitri questions.

"We have been given time to train up. I will help in that regard. I was trained by the Sidhe warriors so that I may in turn train you. If you all are willing, the Vampires will come at night and spar with you. Trust me, your families and loved ones, changed or not have nothing to fear from them. They have been out within the normal human population for months working night shifts. As for when it will happen, when we're contacted, we'll let you know so we can coordinate." Nickolai informs the group.

"Will you excuse us a moment while we converse with each other?" Dimitri requests.

Nickolai, Drew and I all nod in agreement and head out toward the door.

"Come back!" Dimitri calls out to us in a half laugh.

We didn't even make the door, but turn around in

confusion.

"Everyone seems to be in agreement. I barely had my question out before they were agreeing to this alliance." Dimitri laughs out.

I grin. Morcant won't know what hit him with all three groups at his throat.

CHAPTER 30

Rob

I walk down the corridor towards her suite. I wonder what she needs so urgently. Before I knock on the door, Braelomdrel walks up from the opposite direction and stops.

"She called you too?" I ask.

He nods quickly. A sure smile on his face. One I wish to wipe off.

I knock on the door and Amberley answers quickly. She motions both of us to come in and closes the door behind us. Amberley leads us into the sitting room where Avalon is. Avalon motionlessly sits on the couch, her eyes vacant.

"Are you alright?" Amberley asks Avalon gently.

"I'm fine, just lost in thought I guess." Avalon responds with a smile.

I raise my eyebrow at her. I know that look all too well. She glances over at me, for some reason she seems to want her visions to be kept secret from Braelomdrel. I wonder why but say nothing and nod.

"So what do you need of us?" Braelomdrel asks curiously.

"I would like to pick your brains but also to ask both of you to accompany me back to Earth." Avalon replies.

I laugh as the look of disgust and then confusion passes over Braelomdrel's face.

"Sorry, I forget my phrases sound odd here." Avalon giggles out.

Avalon then shows us her necklace. I am stunned. The dragon has moved again, and in its lower claw is the blue Stone of Truth. I did not think we would get to this so soon. I was hoping for more time! I look at Braelomdrel and he seems to be reacting the same as I.

"Now that I have the first piece it is time to start finding the rest. I have a clue to the second but no idea where to start. That is where I need you, Rob." Avalon looks to me.

"Anything." I say without hesitation.

I hope she does not see through my eagerness. She knows I will do anything for her, as is my duty. I do not know if she knows the full extent of my feelings for her.

"I was told to seek someone out at a well whose waters run red. Do you have any idea of where that is?" Avalon asks me.

"There are two that come to mind. Do you have anything else that might narrow it down?" I reply looking down at her. I have a pretty good guess where we will be going. If the next piece is the sword anyway.

"I was told to seek Deverril there." Avalon replies and looks at both of us.

Braelomdrel still looks lost. I laugh inwardly. I haven't seen Deverril in over a century, hopefully he is still there.

"I know exactly where we need to go." I grin. "Tomorrow we will go on a trip to the UK. It has been a long time since I was last there, but it will be nice to go back. I would like Senna and Zephyr to come with us, if you do not mind."

A look of surprise passes on her face for a moment. "Is there any particular reason you want the two of them to join us?" Avalon asks.

"Senna is very skilled in weapons and would be an excellent addition in case we have need. Zephyr is the best healer we have. Besides, he has been itching to get out of the Sidhe for a bit." I chuckle.

Avalon nods.

~*~

I catch Bain out in the courtyard, surprised he hasn't gone back to his hermitage. Bain grins as I approach.

"I thought you might have need of me still." Bain mindspeaks.

I nod.

"I have not had the chance to test the ability in the Princess since she was Awakened. I do not want to risk her life and any others if she tries to bring a group through the veil. I do not know if she is even capable of that yet." Bain explains.

"I understand. Besides, it probably helps if she has been to the place we need to go before." I tell him and he nods.

"Where is it that you need to go and who is coming along?" Bain inquires.

"Avalon, Braelomdrel, Zephyr, Senna and I need to get to the UK. Do you remember any of the places nearby that we can be dropped off at?"

"I do, however, it is in Ireland. Near the old stone." Bain informs me.

"Great! Could you do me a quick favor and pop us over to the house? I would like for a few to join us in Ireland." I request.

Bain nods and extends his hand. I grasp it and find myself standing next to Bain in the living room of Carl's house.

I look around. Melanie is standing oddly still. She turns around quickly and then relaxes as recognition dawns on her. Worry quickly spreads across her face.

"Avalon is fine. It was a bit touch and go for a few moments but she pulled through. In a month's time we will meet you, Drew and Nickolai in Dublin. We have something to retrieve in the UK and I would like to have a few extra hands with me just in case." I tell her.

"With what funds exactly?" Melanie inquires. "We aren't

wealthy around here you know."

I grin at the haughtiness creeping back into her tone.

"I will arrange for the flights with funds at Avalon's disposal. I just need to use the computer and make the arrangements." I state quickly.

"Oh!" Melanie looks slightly taken back.

I make my way to Carl's computer, still in his office and turn it on. It hums to life and the home screen lights up. I pull up the browser and search for airlines that will fly from Denver to Dublin. Aer Lingus airlines pops up in the search engine. I pull out a drawer in Carl's old desk and release the catch inside it. The emergency credit card.

I will have to remember to pay that back later. Quickly, I book three flights to Dublin from Denver and print out the tickets. I stash the card back in the desk and grab the paper tickets on the printer. I walk back into the kitchen and hand the tickets to Melanie. She looks down at the papers and her mouth pops open.

"I hope you all have your passports. If not, you have a month to obtain them." I say quickly and walk back toward Bain who is sitting in the living room.

"Before you go, Katya's community has agreed to join into an alliance with us. We go back tonight to start training them." Melanie bursts out.

"Well done. We will need them, but I am hoping they will have enough time to train before then." I say and grasp the hand that Bain extends out.

I see Melanie nod before the inside of the house fades and the courtyard of the Palace once again surrounds us.

CHAPTER 31

Braelomdrel

I wait patiently as Rob leaves the room. Amberley takes one look at me and quietly leaves the room as well. I sit down beside Avalon and turn to face her.

"Do you care to share why you were gazing off into nothing when we came in? It seems as though everyone else knows but me." I implore.

"I didn't want you thinking I'm crazy. I just see things, sometimes when I'm not trying to at all." Avalon explains quickly.

"I know a few people that have the sight. I do not think you are crazy. Maybe I can help with solving some of your visions if you would share them with me. I am pretty good at interpretations." I smile at her.

"I have had a few that are unsettling to me. Some before

the Awakening and during. I had another after obtaining the stone for the Key." She says quietly.

"Who else knows about them?" I ask gently.

"My visions? Well Amberley, Rob, Nickolai, a couple of people in Colorado, Aislinn and now you that I'm aware of. I want to keep the number small." She said grudgingly.

I try not to take an affront to the last comment. I can understand why she feels this way.

"Well how about we start on one that is not so unsettling. Tell me about that one." I coax.

"It was about you, and not about you. It doesn't make much sense. Then it changed and someone was yelling at my grandfather." She says slowly, albeit confusingly.

I sit back in surprise. "When did you see this?"

"The first night in the Sidhe, before we arrived at the Palace." She replies.

"Do you always see glimpses of the future?" I query.

"Not always. Lately what I see and hear doesn't make any sense. It is as if it might be part of the future and the present." She answers cautiously.

"What do you mean you hear things? You mean apart from your visions?" I ask in worry.

"Yes, but it is hard to explain. It's like mindspeak, but not. I don't know who is talking to me. I don't initiate the conversation, he does." She says warily.

"When was the last time he spoke with you? When it did not feel like one of your visions." I question her.

"That is another thing. When I think it is a vision, it isn't. We have conversations. It isn't one way information. There have been two so far. The first was right after our picnic, the second was during my Awakening Ceremony. He helped pull me through the fire within. I don't think he means me any harm. I have searched to try and find the voice that has invaded my mind more than once; I've come up empty." She explains.

I have no words for this. It is considered rude to mindspeak to someone without an introduction. Who would be so bold as to do this to our Princess? It is something I will need to consult with Mother on later. Whoever it is, saved her, I have to give him that. I do not approve of his methods.

"Have you seen him in your visions? I know more of the people than you do; perhaps I can guess who he is." I offer.

"I have seen a distant glimpse of him but not with much detail. Brown hair with flecks of gold and green eyes. He seemed tall, but then many are compared to me." Avalon says.

"That is not much to go on." I admit. "I will ask around discretely."

Avalon nods.

"What was bothering you when we came in?" I ask.

"That one I have an idea on already. Two different people that look very similar, like they could be related, but

I'm not sure how."

"Who?" I ask.

"*Morcant and my grandfather!*" Avalon mindspeaks to me.

My eyes open wide in surprise. It was the last thing I expected her to say.

"Are you sure?" I choke out.

"Why else would I see both of them together like that?" She asks.

"To be honest, I have no clue. I will help you piece it together after this is over, okay?" I entreat her.

Avalon nods. An odd look crosses her face momentarily.

"I have a favor to ask you." Avalon says softly.

"Name it." I reply.

"Teach me how to fly." Avalon's eyes brighten with excitement. "I need to learn, and you can teach me. I don't want to be useless with wings. I must know how to use them."

"Alright, have Amberley outfit you with some clothes that will adapt and meet me in the garden in an hour." I grin. This could be fun.

~*~

A light wind picks up and blows some loose hair in my face. The movement of air feels good on my bare back and chest. I do not understand how any Angel could pretend to be human for so long. Our lack of getting cold or hot, should be give-a-ways. Unless the Angel is a gifted actor.

"Brae!" Avalon calls out, running up to me from the castle. Her presence pulls me out of my own thoughts and into the present.

I smile down at her. Her white hair is weaved into a braid that lays between her shoulder blades. I motion for her to turn to examine the black tank top she is wearing. She turns for me, showing off the small almost invisible slits Amberley expertly hid within the shirt. I look her over once more. The figure hugging tank top and jeans pull at my gut.

"So how does this work? How can I fly?" She asks impatiently.

"Well first, let's see how well you can control them. Make them appear and then disappear." I said briskly.

Avalon stands in front of me. Her face contorting in various ways. At one point her face turns red. I cannot help it. I laugh out loud.

"What exactly are you doing?" I manage to get out while laughing.

"Trying to get my wings out of course." She says irritably.

"Okay, well this is not magic. They do not just magically appear. Your wings are a part of you, another extension of the body. Just like a limb, you have to move them." I walk towards her back and place my hands inside the slits of her shirt. "Push my hands away. Visualize, and push me away. You do not need to hold your breath like before. Breath deep and concentrate."

I stand there a moment. She can do this, they have been out before. I start to feel her back bulge slightly under my hands, then the skin changes to feathers, muscle and bone.

"It burns!" Avalon cries out.

"I know, keep going! The faster you can do this the less it hurts." I tell her. The feathers fade, and the bulges subside as my hands are back on smooth skin. "Why did you stop?" I demand.

"It frickin hurts! I just need a minute. Then I can try again." Avalon whimpers.

"Nothing in life, especially for those like us, is easy. You have to grab onto what you want, embrace it and never let go. Do not wimp out at pain. Push through it and then hold onto the gift you are given for dear life." I tell her.

Avalon looks up at me and glares. I am not sure if she is mad at me or herself at this moment.

"You're right." Avalon turns her back to me. "Again!" She barks.

I place my palms on her back and wait. The bulges form again and feathers take the place of skin. I can hear her breathing through the pain. A large groan and yell comes next and my body slams down onto the paving stones before I realize what happened. I look up and see Avalon, a look of triumph on her face, white wings spread in victory. I grin.

"After the first time, with all the pain, it made me realize something." She says.

"What was that?" I ask.

"Of the Angels I have seen, to reveal their wings, none have ever done so, slowly. It is always a quick burst." She smiles. "You were right, sort of. It hurts less, well it hurts the same but just not as long."

I nod.

"When you were giving me your pep talk just then. You weren't just talking about wings. What is it that you want to grab onto and hold on for dear life?" Avalon eyes level at me, as if she could see right into my very being.

I look at her for a moment. Could she really not know or is this a game girls play where they want you to say it out loud?

I stand up and dust the dirt from by backside. "No, I was not. The same principle applies though." I say, dodging her question. I will not play that game.

She looks at me a moment longer before shaking off whatever was on her mind. "So what is next?"

"Next, we shall see if you can get yourself into the air and stay up there." I grin. My wings sprout forth and I jump into the air. I fly upwards, pumping my wings hard, then flare them out and glide, slowly descending. I bring my body perpendicular to the ground and call down to her.

"Time to show me what you can do, sweetheart!" I say in haughty tone. I shock myself at the last word but watch as her posture changes slightly.

Avalon, with her wings tucked in tight, jumps up into the air. Her wings flap awkwardly in the air before she falls. Hmm. Maybe I should let her glide first. I tuck my wings in again and plummet toward the ground, then spread them out just before landing, to avoid a hard impact.

"Show off." Avalon mutters. I look at her and smile. Her expression is not one of envy but amusement.

"Sorry. To be honest, I have never taught anyone how to fly before. Most of us that can fly, learned at a very young age. How about we try gliding first. I will not let you fall. I promise." I hold my hand out to her.

Avalon takes my hand and stands close. I bring her closer into an embrace and jump. I pump my wings even harder than before, given the extra weight and bulk of her seemingly useless wings. I stretch my wings out to let us float down at a slow steady pace.

"Okay, spread your wings and feel the air flow around them. Do exactly what I am doing." I say, moving her out away from my body.

Avalon spreads her wings and the air current catches them. Her body raises suddenly and I lose my grip. She yelps and I grab a hold of her hands. I pull her closer to me again.

"I promised you. I would not let you fall. Trust me, okay?" I look her in the eye.

"Okay." Avalon says softly, her body trembling slightly beneath my hands.

"Okay. Now, I want you to try to flap your wings at the same time." I tell her moving my hands to take hers.

Avalon nods, and clumsily starts to flap her wings. I hold onto her hands tight to keep her steady. Her strokes become stronger and hold to a steady rhythm. I match her rhythm with my own so she does not start to carry my weight.

"I'm ready for you to let go now." She says.

"Are you sure?" I ask.

Avalon nods in response. I let go of her hands slowly, keeping my hands within reaching distance should she need me. Her face lights up in excitement, after realizing she is flying on her own. I watch, as if through her eyes, realizing how wonderful flying is for the first time. She tries turns and glides, whooping and yelling in excitement. I laugh.

A strong wind hits me and I adjust to compensate without thinking. Avalon, thirty feet away, falters and plummets losing all control. She screams in panic. I can see that she is struggling to correct herself but just like a baby bird, does not have the strength and practice to manage it. Tucking my wings in, I dive after her. I grasp a hold of her and realize the ground is incredibly too close for comfort. Pulling her into a strong embrace, I open up my wings to slow our descent. It is not enough. I turn my body to protect her just before hitting the ground hard on my back. I feel the skin split open and feathers rip from my wings. I grit my teeth against the pain, groaning.

I relax my hold on Avalon and access her to see if she is injured.

"Are you alright?" I manage to get out. She looks at me as if I have just asked a stupid question.

"Are you?" Avalon asks, the worry clear on her face. Her hands softly roam my body checking for injuries.

"I will survive. My only concern was for your safety, any injury I sustain is of little consequence." I inform her, grunting in pain while trying to sit up. I feel the skin stretch at the tears. I retract my wings, knowing they will heal on their own since there is no break.

Avalon, sitting now in my lap, looks directly into my eyes. Before I can say anything more, her lips crush upon mine. The pressure eases a bit and her kisses are feather light caresses. I move to hold her in my arms, but the pain that shoots up my back makes a pained sound come from my mouth. Avalon pulls back, the look of shock and of concern distort her features.

"Never say your well-being is of little consequence. Your well-being matters to me. What happens to you matters." Avalon says, but still looks a bit shaken.

I wonder why. She shifts and removes herself from me. Avalon offers me a hand to assist me up. It is a sweet gesture to be sure. She cannot actually pull me up, I inwardly chuckle. I stand up with little assistance and she motions for me to turn around. I oblige.

"Oh crap! This looks really bad." Avalon blurts out.

"You need to work on your filter." I laugh. "Your bedside manner is horrible. I will go see Zephyr and will be fine in the morning." I reassure her.

"Would you like me to join you? Do you need help?" Avalon asks, still worried.

"My legs are not broken." I smile down at her. "Honestly, I will be okay. It is getting late. Go get some sleep, I promise everything will be fine." I bend down and kiss her gently, ignoring the pain in my back.

"I'll see you in the morning then." Avalon says in resignation.

~*~

My small duffel bag is packed, along with the correct currency for the area we are going to. I am sure Rob will have some in any case but it is safer just to have a backup. With nothing left but to sleep on a sore back, I sit in front of the bowl of water. Before I can call out her name, my mother's face appears before me in the water below.

"I had a deep urging that you need to speak with me?" My mother asks. The look on her face is one of curiosity.

"Avalon has visions!" I blurt out.

"It is not so unusual for our people to have an ability like that. Please tell me you have more than that." The disappointment on my mother's face is clear.

"She has this notion that Morcant and Finvarra are related. Is there truth to this? Does Finvarra have a younger brother?" I ask her.

"He has a brother, older or younger I do not know. They look nothing alike. The only offspring he has had was Trieva. It is more plausible Avalon thinks they are related because she dislikes them both." My mother reasons.

"She also mentioned someone mindspeaking to her during her Awakening Ceremony. That he invaded her mind and talked her through it. I want to know who it is. Do you know anyone that can force mindspeak before the Awakening has happened?" I demand from her.

"It is possible she heard the voice during her transition, so it could be anyone that can mindspeak. She does not recognize the voice?" My mother asks, intrigued.

"She heard the same voice before her Awakening Ceremony. Avalon says when she hears it, it is like mindspeak, but it feels different." I explain.

"She has never met the person?" My mother raises a brow.

"Not that she has admitted to. The fact that she says when it happens it feels like a vision and also like mindspeak, but it is not; it is different. That has me worried." I admit.

"An interesting puzzle to be sure." My mother says. "I must consult with some others and get back to you."

"I will be going back to the old country tomorrow with Avalon and the Fairy Prince. I will contact you when we are back." I blurt out before she disappears.

"It has begun then? When did she find the first piece?" My mother questions me.

"This morning. She found the Stone of Truth hidden within the stone pillar." I answer.

"Excellent. Protect her in this journey, it may have positive outcomes for you." My mother says with a wink.

I nod. I was not about to share my experience this evening with her. That was private. The image of my mother on the water fades.

~*~

A light rap on my door wakes me. A small amount of light shines through the window and into my room. I get up, dress quickly and grab my duffel. I open the door and Amberley stands in the hallway. The sight of her multitude of colors startles me a bit. Why is she here and not with Avalon? Immediately, my mind starts racing and preparing for the worst.

"Amberley! Where is Avalon?" I demand.

"Calm yourself!" Amberley rolls her eyes. "I needed to wake Sleeping Beauty, because the others are waiting on him."

Realization dawns after a moment. "Are they still in the courtyard?"

"Yes." Amberley says with a laugh as I start running.

The hallways blur together as I make a mad dash to the courtyard. If only I could spread my wings and fly there. I would get there so much faster; the hallways are too cramped for that. I race through the doors to the courtyard and skid to a stop trying not to run into the wall that is Bain.

"*Everyone ready now?*" Bain asks with a smirk for me, then glances at Avalon, Rob, Senna and Zephyr.

We all nod in unison. Avalon glances at me, the worried look still on her face. I wink at her and she nods with a small smile. Suddenly, a large shimmering gateway forms in the center of the courtyard beckoning us.

CHAPTER 32

Nickolai

Working with the Community has made me realize what I've been missing out on. Every day there is a sense of camaraderie and something bigger than myself. Every time I'm there I get to spend more time with Katya. She accepts my past mistakes and makes me feel desired. I can see a life here, within the Community, with Katya.

I wonder, though, how many will go to the Sidhe once this is all done. The Were can't unless things change but the Fae always can. The Fae bring another level to the community, even though the ones here have grown up in the Sidhe. Their skills aren't as finely honed.

The ring of the doorbell brings me out of my wondering. My bag is barely packed! I quickly grab stuff out of drawers and start shoving them inside the bag. I'm sure where we will be going will have toiletries. Leaving the bag on my bed, I leave the room and find Katya waiting for me in the living room. The worry in her eyes is as plain as day.

"Do you really have to go?" Katya asks, her arms wrapping around me in a warm embrace.

"I do. I need you to do us all a favor while we are gone, if you're willing?" I implore.

"It depends what it is." Katya replies with a slight grin.

"Everyone here is comfortable with you. I would like you to take control of things while we are gone. Is that something you would feel comfortable doing?" I ask her softly and ply her with a kiss.

"Oh I suppose." She says with a small giggle.

"Good. You have my cell in case I need to be reached. I will miss you." I envelop her in a hug, picking her up in my arms. "I can't promise this will be the last time I'll have to leave you behind. You will always be with me." I kiss her again.

The front door opens and a throat clears. Katya and I grin at each other and look to Drew standing in the hallway.

"Time to go. I'll look after him, don't worry Kat. Then you both can get back to whatever." Drew says as he waggles his brows.

I laugh. "You know how ridiculous that looks?" I ask.

"Yep. Now let's go." Drew motions to the door. "Melanie! It's time to go! Get your sassy ass outside!" Drew yells.

Katya cracks up and I smile. I will miss her so much while we are gone. Melanie runs by us quickly flashing a smile complete with fangs and tags Drew on the butt as she leaves the house. I glance at Drew for a moment.

"I love that girl!" Drew laughs and chases after Melanie.

"I will call when we land, okay?"

Katya nods as I set her down. I give her a quick kiss and walk after Drew and Melanie.

~*~

The plane touches down, and I glance at my phone now that we are in Dublin. With the exception of the layover in London's Heathrow, the flights were uneventful. I'm tired though. I have never been able to sleep on planes. Melanie didn't have much of a problem. We got on the plane before dawn. Melanie had just enough time to situate herself before passing out. The sun was up through our entire trip. I have to admit though, watching Drew carry her from one flight to the other was entertaining. His excuse to anyone that asked about Melanie; she was drugged up for fear of flying! No one can quite shout out 'Comatose Vampire coming through, make way!'

I text Katya instead of call as I walk to the rental desk to pick up the SUV. I pick up the keys and chuckle to myself as Drew follows behind me, still carrying Melanie. I look back at the directions in my phone of where we are to meet the others. Why Rob has us meeting him at the Hill of Tara, I have no idea. It's really not near anything but a couple small towns.

Outside of the airport we arrive at the rental lot and find one SUV sitting in the lot, a copper Range Rover. According to the clerk, SUV's aren't highly sought after here. She looked at me funny when there were only three of us and one was being carried.

I opened the back door for Drew and then climbed into the driver's seat. Thank god for automatic, a standard would have been a nightmare. I plug my phone into the USB port in the car and turn navigation on. Checking to make sure Drew and Melanie are situated I backed out, and drive to the exit.

As I pull onto the highway labeled M2, Melanie groans slightly from the back seat.

"Welcome back to the world of the living!" I call back with a snicker.

"Oh. Ha. Ha." Melanie retorts and rolls her eyes. "Woah!" She exclaims while looking out the window.

"Melanie, there are going to be some farms out where we are going. If you need to, grab one of the animals there later." I call out to the back of the car.

"I think I've got my needs figured out by now." Melanie snaps.

"Babe, I know you just woke up, but chill a tad. Okay?" Drew admonishes her.

"Sorry Nickolai." Melanie says quickly.

I nod and decide its best that she is left alone for now. We pass by several rural towns as we travel northwest on the

M2. For the most part the land is rather flat and reminds me of parts of Colorado. I turn left onto the small rural road labeled L1002. Not long after that it feels like we are traveling through a green tunnel. On both sides of the severely small country road are tall bushes, shrubs and trees. Some have grown up and over the road.

After a few more turns we end up on an even smaller country road. I didn't know it was even possible. It doesn't look like two cars could even fit next to each other on this road. The road starts to climb uphill. Low stone walls covered with greenery line the road. Only patches of the old stone is visible. Slowly the road opens up and filters into a parking lot for The Hill of Tara.

I pull into a space while Melanie slathers herself with sunscreen. I look up at the sky. The cloud cover is still heavy and should provide her with some protection. The sun won't be down for a few hours yet. I get out of the car and stretch my legs a bit. It wasn't a bad drive for forty minutes.   Drew and Melanie join me on the sidewalk. We head past the gated entryway with the low stone walls walk towards the old church.

We fan out and look around the old church including the small cemetery. No sign of Rob or Avalon anywhere. The walkway continues on past the church and opens up into what looks like fields. Drew and Melanie join back up with me. We walk towards the fields. There is a light trail through the fields towards what looks like a round hill. The area is very hilly but only in certain places.

We follow the path. Due to the time of day, we are the

only ones here. It is probably around dinner or closing time if I had to guess. The path stops in front of the round hill. There is an entrance into the mound which is surrounded by built up stone and gated off to discourage entry. From the condition of the gate, it looks like it has been here for quite some time. I'm curious as to what this place is. I walk up to the sign posted nearby only to see a shimmer out of the corner of my eye. A very familiar shimmer.

A gateway appears just on this side of the gate in the mound. Rob steps out first. I look around, checking for any reactions to what is going on. Besides the four of us, there is no one. Two people emerge next, and a grin spreads across my face. Zephyr and Senna, no doubt added to our party for their special gifts. A small female steps through next, her white hair is almost unnaturally bright against the all black outfit. A tall man, the one I recognize from the Great Hall and the small room Rion took me to before leaving the Sidhe, follows the woman and the gate closes.

I look back at the woman with the white hair and she raises her head to meet my gaze. My mouth drops open in shock.

"Do I really look that bad?" Avalon laughs lightly.

I look to Drew and Melanie, their expressions are the same as mine.

"No, you look stunning, but this is not how you normally dress." I gesture at her. "Plus, I don't think any of us were expecting such a drastic change in your hair and eyes." I blurt out.

"I'm still not used to it. This only happened two days ago. As to the outfit, this is Amberley's work. You should see the extra armor she packed away in here." Avalon says patting her pack.

"So you know what your Mother's family is then?" I ask her.

"Oh yes. I knew before choosing to go through with this. It isn't something I can share with you all right now, out in the open." Avalon says as she ties her hair back. She pulls the hood up on the hoodie she is wearing to help cover her hair. She turns and faces Rob. "Rob, I would like to see the original stone before we go."

Rob nods. "Follow me." He heads to the south, toward the hilly areas of the field. We walk up and find ourselves at the top of a hill. There is a grave marker and a large stone pillar surrounded by stones laid into the earth around it. Avalon bypasses the grave marker and heads to the large pillar and touches it lightly. A slight tone sounds.

I look around to see where it is coming from. I notice Drew and Melanie are doing the same. Avalon turns slightly and I notice something I'd never seen before. A dragon pendant is around her neck, its wings slightly outstretched. The dragon surrounds a circle and a trinity knot. One of its feet is clutching a bright blue stone that seems to be glowing. She takes her hand off the pillar and the tone stops, the stone's glow also fades.

"Interesting. There must be some slight connection to the pillar on the stone still." Rob says quietly as some more tourists join us on top of the hill.

"I don't know about you guys, but I could eat, a lot, right now." Drew says loudly, earning a few chuckles from the tourists around us.

"There is a small cafe here. We can grab a bite to eat there." Rob says, then looks quickly at Melanie.

"I'll be fine. There are plenty of sheep around." Melanie sighs and gestures to the sheep grazing on the grass near the mound.

CHAPTER 33

Avalon

Rob leads the way as the rest of us follow sans Melanie. I feel bad that she has to be left out of things that are so normal to the rest of us. Something Rob said back in Colorado suddenly pops in my brain. I wonder if it is possible. If Sidhe citizens can be stripped of their current abilities, could the changes in Melanie also be reversed? I will have to remember to mention this later to see what can be done for her. The way Drew and Melanie seem to revolve around each other, it would not be fair to leave her like that, if it can be helped.

I keep feeling like someone is staring at me as we continue to walk. I don't want to turn to see who it is. Is it Nickolai or Brae?

Nickolai was only able to send a letter before he left and it kind of echoed my thoughts. We were done, but I'm not sure he got closure. Does he still feel that way or did seeing me again bring something back for him? I truly hope he has moved on. I just can't see him the same way I once did. I want for him to be happy. He deserves that at least for what he has gone through. I don't blame him for my father's death. I never really did. I was just hurt and angry.

My thoughts shift to focus on Brae. I still can't believe I kissed him last night. It wasn't just because of what happened. He has been so nice and thoughtful since I came to live in the Sidhe. He has been a very close friend and easy to talk with. Brae also doesn't make me feel stupid because I don't know the things that most do. I want to learn more about Brae and his family. I like what I've seen so far.

I don't know what to do. However, I know what I'm not going to do. I'm not going to keep myself for some stranger I don't know and still have yet to see. There is no telling who this stranger is and when I will see him, but I'm not about to let some guy dictate to me how my future will be.

Rob leads us into Maguire's Cafe. The small cafe is decorated with paintings and various art. Small and large wooden table and chairs fill the dining area of the cafe. Off to the side of the cafe is a gift shop, which I doubt I'll have time to window shop through. The smells of fresh baked goods hang in the air. My mouth starts watering almost instantly. It smells so good in here!

We gather at a long table near a stone work wall that runs the entire length of the room. Senna takes the seat at my left and Rob the one on the right. Brae sits down in front of me and Zephyr across from Senna. Nickolai and Drew sit together across from Rob. The seat next to Rob empty, in case Melanie comes in to join us. I watch in fascination on how the seating arrangements were made without even speaking, not even through mindspeak. I knew why the seating arrangements were as they were. I was being protected.

"Nickolai, may I borrow your phone for a moment?" Rob asks after the waitress leaves.

"Sure, but why?" Nickolai asks while pulling his cell from his pocket.

"I need to secure lodging and reservations for the ferry for the next leg of this trip." Rob states matter-of-factly, and takes the offered phone.

"We aren't staying in this area?" I ask Rob out of curiosity and so that he doesn't zone out into the phone.

"No, this was just an easy transport point for Bain, since he remembers it. That is why I had the others meet us there. The stone used to be on the mound, I am not sure why it was moved to another hill, but whatever. Our next stop is in England, but I need to secure lodging and the ferry. Lodging won't be difficult, I just have to locate the old family that is loyal to the Sidhe near Glastonbury. It is the travel from here, to catch the ferry and then the drive to our lodging that may prove difficult." Rob blurts out while concentrating hard on the small screen of Nickolai's phone.

"Why would the travel be difficult?" I ask.

Rob looks up from the phone and stares at me. Crap! I just asked a stupid question that has an obvious answer, then it dawns on me. If the ferry doesn't keep running late enough or doesn't start early enough, Melanie may be caught in the day light. Even if the windows are tinted in the back of the vehicle they got, it won't keep the sun's rays from coming through the windshield or front windows.

"Never mind." I mutter.

Rob abruptly stands up from his chair, pushes it into the table and walks over to a quiet corner while punching in a phone number. He stands in the corner for a time, chatting jovially with whoever is on the other end before walking back over to the table.

"Well we have a problem." Rob starts, all our heads turn toward him, as he sits back down.

"Lodging is all set. We will be staying at a Marie's. She runs a small bed and breakfast near the Tor. The problem is, if we cannot make the last ferry for the night which leaves in an hour and a half, the next one is at 1:55 tomorrow morning. The drive from Holyhead to our lodging is a five hour drive. We will not make it before the sun rises, if we do not make this last ferry. I will review what options we have should we need them and let you all know." Rob states.

"Options?" I look quickly at Rob.

"Well, we can speed like a bat out of hell. I can try to project my invisibility around us and the car, I have never done that before, so it is a risk. Only other option is for you to take her." Rob advises.

"Bain made it clear, I wasn't to group travel yet. I know I've accidentally done it already, but he says we were lucky nothing happened

to us, since I didn't create a gateway like he does. I don't even know how to create a gateway. Plus, I don't know where we are going!" I mindspeak back.

"Would a picture help? Even if it is last resort?" Rob questions.

"Maybe. Except for flukes when I was young and when I transported you and Nickolai after the lake, I have always physically been to a place before I've tried traveling to it." I'm sure the worry is showing slightly on my face, and notice Brae looking at me quizzically. I shake my head.

"For now, we will try to avoid it then." Rob states.

I feel a tentative pressure within my mind, different from Rob. I lower my resistance to whoever is trying to talk, ready to throw it back up if needed.

"Avalon? Are you okay?" Braelomdrel asks tentatively.

"Yes, I'm fine. Rob and I were having a discussion of traveling. I haven't learned how to make a gateway yet, and Bain doesn't want me traveling with a group without learning how to make a gateway first. I wouldn't want to risk anyone doing it wrong."

Braelomdrel nods just as the waitress arrives with a tray laden with food. Plates are passed around and everyone digs in. As soon as the waitress leaves, Rob stops eating and clears his throat, drawing our attention.

"If we miss the last ferry tonight, I have only one viable solution and it is not the greatest. For the drive from the Ferry to Little Orchard, whatever I can do to help keep us all hidden while speeding, will be done. If we have anything to cover Melanie with should that not work, get them out before we leave. Eat quickly please."

We eat our meals in a hurry and leave, with payment plus a generous tip on the table. Melanie waves at us from a large SUV. We all walk quickly to the vehicle. Drew fills Melanie in and asks her a question that I don't quite hear. She nods.

"How are we on time?" I ask.

"I have entered the destination into the GPS. Everyone get in quickly, we barely have enough time to make it, let alone purchase our fare." Rob responds quickly as he buckles himself into the driver's seat without checking to see if anyone else wants to drive.

Rob sticks his hand out to Nickolai for the keys. Nickolai hands him the keys and then walks to the passenger seat and gets in. The rest of us pile into the back of the SUV. I expected Senna, Zephyr and Braelomdrel to say more about how different this is from the Sidhe, but they don't. It almost seems like they are familiar with it. I chalk it up to more information that needs to be delved into later.

Rob pulls quickly out of the parking lot before I'm even able to put my seat belt on. I glare at him for a moment and Senna, catching my reaction, chuckles slightly.

"He does tend to get focused on one thing too easily and forgets some small things like seat belts when on a mission. You will get used to it." Senna says quietly.

Well that answers my previous question but brings up others. What kind of missions have they gone on before? I know they are all extremely old but what have they been doing for their "missions"?

We reach the ferry dock in record time but it looks like the ferry is full. Hoping we still might have a shot, Rob and I approach the ticket counter while the others wait in the SUV.

"I'm sorry folks, but we just sold out. The last vehicle just loaded on. It's a shame, but you will have to wait until the next one at 1:55 tomorrow morning." The guy at the ticket counter says.

Rob nods. "I'll take the 1:55 fare then."

We walk back to the SUV. I'm hoping I don't have to transport Melanie, that Rob can make this work.

"Might as well get as much rest as we can." Rob says to the group as we get back into the SUV. "Melanie, would you mind waking us up so that we can get onto the 1:55 ferry?"

Melanie nods.

~*~

The ferry docks at Holyhead, it is really too late to see anything. My first experience of England is a real yawner. I'm a bit disappointed but we aren't here for site seeing anyway. We slowly exit the ferry with other vehicles and Rob maneuvers us onto the North Wales Expressway to head east. The vehicle begins to accelerate and a pensive look falls across Rob's face. The speed increases for a bit before Rob grunts loudly in exasperation. We start to slow down, and Rob pulls over, stopping the SUV on the side of the road.

"I am unable to drive and concentrate enough to keep us

hidden." Rob admits in disgust as he turns to look back at the others in the vehicle.

"I will drive." Braelomdrel says quickly.

"I would prefer if Nickolai drives. To be frank, I do not know how well you can drive. Or even if you can." Rob states.

Nickolai nods and Braelomdrel says nothing more. The look on Braelomdrel's face shows his displeasure at the slight. Nickolai opens up the rear passenger door and exchanges seats with Rob. I turn back around and feel the breeze being blocked by Rob as he gets into the vehicle. The breeze continues to blow a bit from the driver's door and I look over. Nickolai is just standing there looking at me. I raise my eyebrows and he shakes himself quickly and gets into the driver's seat.

Can we say awkward? I know the last time we were in a vehicle together like this; we were a couple and driving to my dad's house. The thought of my dad brings a large lump to my throat. I check on Rob one last time before closing my eyes. No awkward moments, if he thinks I'm asleep!

I'm rudely awakened by the sounds of sirens and everyone shouting. I look around trying to figure out what is going on. There is a police vehicle behind us with its sirens blaring and lights flashing. Rob was unable to keep us hidden. Crap.

Rob shoves his phone in my face. "See the image there?" He asks quickly.

"Yes. What of it?" I yell back.

"We will not make it with Melanie in the back of the vehicle. We do not have enough items to keep her covered and her looks will spook the officer this late at night." Rob states briskly.

"Marie is already ready and prepared should this need arise. She is waiting for you at this location." Rob says nodding his head directing me back to the phone.

"I don't want to risk killing her." I try to explain.

"Humans tend to fear what they do not understand. It is highly probable, that the officer may shoot us all if he gets spooked. I have faith that you can do this. You need to have faith in yourself. " Rob pleads

I nod and look at the picture with more intensity, trying to ingrain it in my mind. I grasp for Melanie's hand. Her ice cold hand slides onto mine and shocks me for a moment. I look at the picture one last time and toss the phone to Rob. The interior of the vehicle fades into nothing and the only sensory perception I have is of a cold hand clasping tight onto mine. I don't remember ever having this void before when I traveled. My stomach starts to flip in panic.

"I don't feel so well. What is going on?" Melanie cries out as if yelling against wind.

"I don't know!" I shout back.

Then I realize, I've forgotten to keep the image in my mind of where we were going. I quickly try to recall the image, but it is hard. It is there one moment and gone the next. Slowly the nothing starts to flicker and I can see the place we are supposed to go and a shocked woman standing in front of us. The place recedes again and flickers back and I fling Melanie hard at the woman. I see Melanie collide with the woman just before I'm enveloped by the void. My head starts to spin. If I pass out in here what will happen to me? I focus hard on the image in my mind. It flickers back into view and I run. The ground comes up to meet my face as I fall. I hit the grass and a dirt path before all is black again.

CHAPTER 34

Melanie

Talk about rude introductions. Toppling onto some poor woman because Avalon wasn't ready for this. True she got me here, but she didn't come out with me. I want to wait for her but I can feel the onset of dawn approaching. There is nothing I can do to help Avalon now, even if I could.

"I need to go inside. Please." I implore the woman, hoping Avalon got me to the right place and this lady speaks English.

The woman nods and leads me inside. "We have a bed set up down in the cellar. Rob told me all about your particular needs, my dear. You needn't worry about a thing." She says softly.

I nod, hoping I'll actually make it to the bed in time. My eyes grow heavy with each step as I'm being led down into the cellar. As promised off in the corner away from any small windows is a small bed with the covers drawn down.

"I'll have something brought down when you wake for breakfast. We wouldn't want to alarm the neighbors." The woman said with a slight giggle.

I nod and sink into the bed before passing out.

~*~

The sounds of voices above me and the smell of an animal in close proximity are my first indications of being back among the living. I open my eyes and take a look around. Drew sits in a chair near the foot of the bed. Head bent down, touching his chest and a soft snore, makes me smile slightly. A frightened baying noise brings my attention away from Drew. A small goat is tethered to a metal ring secured into the wall. I usually like to hunt my meal, but when traveling, one can't be choosy!

"You made quick work of that." Drew chuckles softly from across the room.

I stop and look at him for a moment. Then the events of last night click into place.

"Avalon is fine. Marie found her out in the yard after she brought you inside. Calm down." Drew says in a reassuring tone.

"Is my face that expressive? Or do you have the ability to read minds too?" I ask quickly.

"It's that expressive. I don't think I'd want to be able to read minds. Just a bit too nosy and personal if you ask me."

Drew says as he envelops me in a hug.

"Quit dawdling down there! I know you both are awake. Get up here we need to go soon!" Nickolai shouts down the cellar stairs.

I laugh. This place almost feels like home.

"What about…" I start to ask.

"Jake will take care of the carcass after we leave." Drew says, cutting me off.

I nod and walk up the cellar stairs into the main part of the house.

I walk into the small sitting room to the left of the kitchen where we entered from the cellar. Rob nods at me and Avalon looks up tiredly, looking slightly relieved. Senna and Zephyr stand at the windows with Braelomdrel talking quietly amongst themselves. Nickolai walks in with the tea service tray in one hand and a tray of cakes in the other. Drew moves to help him place them on the table set against the south wall. I sit down to wait, while the others get their tea and cakes.

Oh! If only I could be human today and have tea and cakes too! I chuckle to myself. The old me would have never, ever, said that. It is funny, the things people miss when they can't have them. I already know what it would taste like to me. Dirt. I sigh softly to myself.

"At least you can't get fat." Drew snickers softly as he sits down next to me on the sofa.

I glare at him. He is right. Dang it.

Rob clears his throat. "We will be going out to the well today. There is an old friend there we need to see. He may have an idea of where we must go to look for the sword."

"The well?" I ask in uncertainty. In my mind, I picture a dark, dank well. Like the well from movie, The Ring. I shiver slightly.

"The Chalice Well. Its waters are said to run red." Rob states and Avalon suddenly looks very alert. "The Chalice Well is near the bottom of the Tor, which is also a place of power." Rob continues and looks over at Avalon. Rob stops talking and just stares at her for a while, as if in a private conversation.

"Why couldn't Bain have brought us here?" Avalon asks and shakes her head at Rob.

"Um, would you mind terribly not having private conversations in the middle of ours?" I ask, rather annoyed.

Rob's face flushes crimson for a moment. "My apologies. Avalon said the same as you. Told me it was rude."

I look at Avalon again. I nod at her and she nods back. Maybe we aren't so different after all. She certainly turned out to be a freak just like me. Ha!

"Bain knows Tara well, especially the Mound of Hostages as it is called now. He did not spend time here." Rob says matter-of-factly.

"What is so special about the mound?" Avalon asks.

"The mound was built after your people moved to the Sidhe. It was built as a passageway to bring more of Earth's unique races into the Sidhe for protection. During the Irish Holidays of Samhain and Imbolc, the interior of the mound is completely lit by sunlight and the passageway into the Sidhe is open for three days." Rob explains.

"That is how your parents came to the Sidhe then?" Nickolai asks.

Rob nods.

"So, when do we leave?" I ask.

"As soon as everyone has had their fill, we will go visit with Glyndwr once the place closes to the public." Rob answers and then calls out. "Marie, did you get the black grease paint I asked for?"

"Yes, I did. I will see to it that everyone is covered." Marie says with a chuckle from the doorway.

"Grease paint?" Avalon asks.

"It's for the wings. They will stand out if not darkened. Avalon, you need to go upstairs and put the rest of your armor on. You are not leaving this house without it." Rob says with authority.

"Nothing like sticking out like a sore thumb. Why did Amberley choose red anyway?" Avalon mutters as she gets up and walks up the stairs.

~*~

We leave the house and head toward the Chalice Well

Gardens as night falls. The stone walls and tall shrubbery look uninviting especially with the frost touching everything. We gather together in an unlit corner near the wall. I wonder how everyone is going to make it inside or if those of us that can jump will be ferrying everyone else over. Before I can speak, Avalon, Zephyr, Braelomdrel and Rob have wings.

Wings! Rob's wings are faint almost sheer. The others, well they look like freaking angels, except that their wings are black. The conversation regarding the black grease paint finally dawns on me. Why did no one tell me angels were real? I look over at Drew and Nickolai. They have the exact same stunned expressions on their faces. I wasn't the only one left out in the dark apparently. I start breathing quicker. Crap, if angels are real that means, God is real. I quickly get down on my knees to pray.

Zephyr, chuckling softly, leans down. "Now is not the best time for that. I am sure God is aware of your epiphany."

The winged ones quickly take off and fly over the wall with ease, leaving the rest of us behind. Senna looks at us and chuckles before jumping over the wall effortlessly. Following her lead, the rest of us jump over the wall and land on a stone pathway. Avalon, Zephyr, Braelomdrel and Rob stand there waiting sans wings. How the hell are they able to do that?

Rob leads us up the pathway. The trees, shrubs and stones are covered in frost, giving a glittery, ethereal glow to the place in the moonlight. We come to a fork in the pathway and Rob hesitates.

"Does your friend know we're coming? Can't you do your mind talk thingy to find out where he is?" I ask.

Avalon snickers. Rob's face turns a slight shade of pink in embarrassment, then nods. He stills for a moment and takes the path to the left. Finally, we come to a many tiered pool of sorts. A glittering, watery form of a man stands in the middle of the lowest pool. My mouth opens in astonishment. Drew pushes his fingers up on my lower jaw.

"Flies." Drew whispers softly and chuckles.

I grin and flash some teeth at him. He smiles back and looks at the form in the water.

"My friend." The form says. "It has been too long."

"Aye, it has, Glyndwr. I am in need of information. I have come in hopes that you might have it and aid us." Rob gestures.

Glyndwr turns and seems to look at the rest of us. He bows slightly to Avalon and then pulls a dead stop when his gaze lands on me.

"You..." Glyndwr's voice stops at a gurgle. "I have not felt your kind in a very long time. You are tainted. Sick."

I look back at Glyndwr in shock.

"You have had Vampires here Glyndwr?" Rob asks in alarm.

"Vampires?" Glyndwr asks, seemingly confused.

"Melanie is a Vampire." Rob advises.

"No. She is tainted. She is a sick, Fuath." Glyndwr corrects him.

"She is Fae?" Rob asks Glyndwr in earnest.

"Yes. I can feel it, but she is tainted. There is something in her blood that shouldn't be." Glyndwr says.

"It sounded like I was just called a dirty name. What is a Fuath?" I ask irritably.

"I meant no disrespect." Glyndwr says apologetically. "I can feel the essence of any water Fae, just like the Heir, here. You are a Fuath. A type of water Fae. A normal Fuath feeds on the blood of others occasionally for heightened power, not to be sustained. You feed on the blood of others to live. That is why you are tainted; sick."

"Is there a way to reverse the taint Glyndwr?" Rob asks.

"I am not sure. You may need to speak with Angeliss, she may know. Is this the answer you were seeking?" Glyndwr asks.

"No. We were surprised by your revelation into Melanie's condition. We got side tracked." Rob replies.

"We are needing to find the Sword of Nuada." Avalon speaks up. "Do you by any chance know where we should look for it?"

Glyndwr's face shows a look of shock and surprise. "I haven't seen that sword in ages. Last I heard, it was given back to the Lady."

"What Lady?" Drew asks.

"The Lady that originally gave the sword to the King. She was the last known keeper." Glyndwr explains.

247

Something about this starts to sound familiar. I look at Avalon and she looks back at me, eyes wide.

"This Lady, did she live near a lake?" Avalon asks.

"She did once. Yes. Now she lives in a small river because the lake dried up hundreds of years ago." Glyndwr replies. "She is not too far from here. She may have it or know where it is now."

"The Sword of Nuada is Excalibur?" Avalon asks for clarification.

"That is another name of the Sword of Nuada, yes." Glyndwr clarifies.

"Holy shit balls!" Drew exclaims.

I glare at him.

"What? I never thought Excalibur was real." Drew says.

"You thought this was real before?" I gesture to all of us.

"Well, not until I met Morcant. I see your point." Drew says quickly.

The group chuckles softly. I just wonder what other surprises are lurking about.

CHAPTER 35

Nickolai

The famed Excalibur. It is still so hard to believe it exists. Though I'm highly curious what the Lady of the Lake looks like. We head back to the bed and breakfast to rest and allow Melanie to get home before she passes out again. I wonder what is going through her mind now that she knows what Glyndwr told us. I worry that she may get her hopes up on a reversal. Since she is actually Fae, part of that was slightly Awakened over a year ago. How the hell did Tripp mess that up so badly?

No wonder she is stronger than any of the other Vampires. Vlad is the only one I know of that is stronger. He just had multiple transfusions of Morcant's blood along with the water. Morcant basically made him his equal. When he left, that was why Morcant couldn't stop him. That is why Morcant started making diluted versions. At least, that is what Tripp told me. I have no clue if that is true or not. With everything that we are finding out now, it is hard to think stories are just tales.

Marie and Jake greet us as we come in, letting us know that food is ready and Melanie's room is waiting. Melanie smiles at Marie and heads down the cellar stairs as the rest of us crowd around the kitchen table like starved teenagers. We load up our plates and sit down with our hosts.

"Do you know your next location in this quest?" Jake asks Rob.

"Glyndwr only mentioned speaking to the Lady in some river near here. What rivers are nearby?" Rob inquires.

"The River Brue is not so far from here. My guess is he wants you to talk to Niniane." Marie replies.

"You know the Lady? What can you tell us about her?" Avalon questions Marie.

"She has been around this area for ages. Always here. She was a Lady when I was just a young lass." Marie turns and looks at Rob. "She ages much like you do, dear."

A knowing look crosses between everyone at the table. The Lady, Niniane, is Fae.

"The last time I spoke with her was almost twelve years ago to the south of the Tor. The river is not what it once was and for the life of me, I can't figure out why she would stay there." Marie shakes her head in sadness.

"Let us all get some sleep. We will need our rest. Who knows what information Niniane will provide to us." Avalon says as she stands from the table.

The rest of the group nod silently. We gather up our dishes and carry them into the kitchen for Marie before being shooed away. I take the stairs two at a time to get to my room. I hadn't gotten that much sleep before our journey into the Chalice Well Gardens. I'm exhausted. I clumsily strip down to my boxers and crawl into the small double bed and pull the covers over me. My head hits the pillow and I'm lost to the world.

~*~

A knock on my door, rouses me from sleep.

"Coming!" I call out. I get out of bed and start to dress. I look back at the bed longingly, wishing to be back in its warmth. I sigh.

I take the stairs quickly back down to the ground floor, finding everyone gathered in the sitting room again with more tea and cakes. Braelomdrel, Zephyr and Senna acknowledge my presence with a quick nod. This time they seem to be more social and not huddled together by the window. I help myself to a cup of tea and small plate filled with tiny cakes from the side board. I sit down across from Drew who is snarfing down cakes faster than I've seen anyone eat in quite some time.

"Breathe man. They aren't running out of food." I tease Drew before biting into one of my cakes.

The strong apple and cinnamon flavors of the cake make my eyes close in enjoyment. No wonder Drew is snarfing these down. They are freaking good! I start to eat faster.

"Hey piggies, slow down." Melanie says with a snort of laughter. "Marie, can I get your recipe for those when we leave?"

"Of course, my dear. You've got to keep these boys fed. They burn through calories like you wouldn't believe." Marie says with a chuckle.

"Marie has made us a map of where she last spoke with Niniane. When you two are finished, we will head out." Avalon says quickly.

"Marie, do you have a bag or something that we can take more for the road?" I politely ask her.

"Already thought of that." Marie chuckles, walks into the kitchen for a moment and then comes back out carrying a small cloth sack full of cakes.

"You are a Godsend." I say, taking the sack from Marie and follow the others out of the front door.

I barely get out of the house before Drew is digging into the sack. I look at him in annoyance.

"Chill it with the eating. There is no way of knowing how long it will take us to find Niniane. Ration, for crying out loud." I state sharply to Drew.

Melanie chuckles.

The eight of us walk south through the surrounding neighborhoods. Abruptly the streets lined with houses stops and starts to spread out with farm land. We keep the main road going out of Glastonbury to our right knowing the road will cross the river. Avalon stops suddenly and looks at Rob. I wish they would just do a group speak thing so we knew what was up. I hate being in the dark.

Rob motions for Avalon to lead. She turns and takes off towards the east, running over the grassy, uneven ground. We all follow after her. The sound of running water hits my ears first and then the smell of a fresh water river reaches my nose. I look around and we are now running parallel to a small waterway. To be honest, it looks like a glorified irrigation ditch. Why would a Fae want to live here?

Avalon slows down and walks towards the river's edge. Out in the middle of the river is a small strip of land and a woman with bright blond hair sits there looking at us. One by one, we jump across and find purchase on the small space without jostling each other.

"I'm sorry to disturb you, but is your name Niniane?" Avalon asks politely.

"I go by many names. Niniane is one of them, yes. How do you know of me? What is it that you want?" She fires questions back at Avalon.

"Glyndwr sent us to you. He said you might be able to aid us in finding what we seek." Avalon says quickly.

"What is it that you seek?" Niniane's eyes narrow.

"I seek the Sword of Nuadu." Avalon replies.

"For what purpose? For fame or fortune? To have Excalibur would be a great boon to anyone." Niniane taunts.

"To help save the world from disaster." Avalon says calmly.

"What disaster? The world as I knew it; disaster has already befallen it." Niniane retorts.

"There is a man that is using the Cauldron to Awaken and turn others against their knowledge and will. He is forcing them to serve him in order to build an army." I speak up.

Niniane turns and looks at me. "A soldier. Do you plan on wielding this sword?" Niniane asks curiously.

"No. I have no need of a sword. Avalon needs it to complete her key." I reply.

"Key? What key?" Niniane turns back to Avalon.

Avalon shoots me a look that for all intent and purposes meant I shouldn't have said that. She slowly removes her necklace from under her shirt, showing the Dragon-Triquetra Pendant holding the bright blue Stone of Truth. Niniane reaches for it and Avalon backs up slightly.

"My apologies, I have not been around people much. May I come closer to inspect it further?" Niniane asks.

Avalon nods and places the pendant on her palm, holding it out to Niniane. Niniane peers down at it, touches the pendant lightly and one of the dragon's legs shifts. I stiffen up. I wasn't expecting the dragon on the necklace to move!

"Ah, I see the truth of it now. You wish to be able to take the Cauldron away from this man. You need a piece of the sword, not the actual sword itself. It may be best that the sword be removed from this world anyway. It hasn't been used in hundreds of years." Niniane says after a few moments.

"Will you tell us where it is?" Rob asks.

"I do not know where it is exactly. It was given to a friend of mine for safe keeping and away from the area of its legend. The one you seek can be found at the Fairy Pools on the Isle of Skye. I bid you safe travels." Niniane says dismissively.

"Would you like to come with us? You can't possibly want to stay here." Melanie asks.

"I am older than any of you know. The last of the Ladies. Once the sword is in your possession my charge will be over. Then, I will join my sisters, who I have missed terribly." Niniane says with a smile.

"Are your sisters in the Sidhe? There are many like you there." Avalon says.

"No, child. My sisters have long since passed on and I will join them soon." Niniane says as she walks toward the water.

We watch in silence as Niniane dips below the water without a sound and is gone.

CHAPTER 36

Avalon

Saying good bye to Marie wasn't easy for most of us. I
want to bring her home to the Sidhe with me. I think Drew
and Nickolai want to bring her back to Colorado with them.
She sent us off with care packages. Melanie with her mini
cake recipe, the guys with extra sacks of cakes. They acted
like they would starve if they didn't have them for the road.
Marie also gave us extra old blanket in order to cover Melanie
with should we run into a daylight problem again. I didn't
want to do another blind travel any time soon and she agreed
that it is probably best.

This time, traveling in the SUV is not so stressful. With
the added protection for Melanie, we did not need to worry
about speeding. We only had to stop once, just north of
Birmingham, for an accident on the M6 highway. I finally got
to drive for a while! Nickolai, Drew and Melanie went off the
main road to stretch their legs and hunt. They made it back to

the SUV just as the rest of us passed the accident.

"How much further do we have to go?" Melanie asks, nodding at the eastern horizon.

Nickolai turns on the screen of his smart phone and checks the GPS Navigator. "About nine hours if we don't run into any more accidents. You will have time for a nice nap. I'm a bit envious."

"I'd trade you if I could. You can take this passing out gig and all that comes with it. I don't think I would mind being a tiger." Melanie retorts.

Melanie settles into the far back seat with Drew. He puts a blanket on himself and then she lays down on him. Drew draws up another blanket on top of Melanie. Within moments she is out and Drew covers her head with the blanket.

~*~

Ten hours and another accident later, I climb down out of the SUV, stiff like an old woman. I stretch out, letting everyone else pile out of the vehicle. A sign reading 'Glumagan Na Sithichean' marks the gravel parking area for the fairy pools, Niniane mentioned.

"Are you sure we are at the right place?" Drew asks.

"That is what the sign says." I say with a smirk.

"Like you can read that!" Drew laughs.

"Open your peepers a bit more. It says Fairy Pools in small letters just underneath it." I say through laughter.

The rest of the group snickers and everyone but Melanie grabs a few cakes with them for the hike. The sky is covered in clouds blocking the light of stars and the moon. I can still see where we are going, but just barely. The sound of our feet crunching on the gravel path fills my ears. I look around, noticing Braelomdrel and Zephyr are having the same difficulty as me. The others seem to notice as well and they pair up with us. Rob taking my arm, Senna taking Zephyr's and Nickolai assisting Braelomdrel.

"We need to cross the river up here. There are stepping stones to cross and it is a bit slick. Be careful." Melanie calls back in warning.

The other two go across first, and then Rob takes me across with Drew behind us. Rob is holding onto me so tightly I don't see how it would be possible to slip. Just as the thought crosses my mind; klutziness strikes again and my foot slips out from under me. Rob lifts us up with his wings before my face is able to plant itself on the stepping stone in front of us.

"Thanks." I say, completely embarrassed.

"I will always protect you." Rob says softly.

I nod, saying nothing more. We continue down the gravel path only to cross yet another river. I have no idea if this is the same river, but it's getting old. We cross without incident and after a little while I can hear the sounds of a waterfall close by. The path leads us down near the waterfall and that is where Drew stops us.

"There is something watching us. I can barely see it, but

the smell is unlike anything I have smelled before." Drew says quietly. "It is near the rocks, in the water."

I grow still and close my eyes. I can feel whatever it is, out there. It isn't a Merrow like Niniane is. I have no idea what it is.

"It can't be. I haven't seen one in over a hundred years. I thought they all died out." Senna says in astonishment.

"What?" Rob asks quickly.

"It's a Water Elf." Senna replies.

"Very good. Now what do you noisy creatures want? I have to deal with tourists all the bloody time. Night is the only time I have to myself!" A high pitched voice calls out over the sound of the waterfall. The form in the water drawing near.

"Niniane sent us. She said you were given the Sword of Nuadu for safe keeping." Senna states firmly.

"It is safe where it is. There is no need for any of you to take it. No one has been able to find it, since I placed the sword over three hundred years ago." The Water Elf replies in kind.

"Actually, I do need it. I was sent to retrieve it." I say quickly.

"Fat chance that. I'd like to see any of you get into water this cold and retrieve the sword from where it is hidden." The Elf laughs heartily.

"If we can, then what?" Melanie challenges.

"If you can. That is a huge if by the way. You can take it back to the Sidhe. Yes, I know what most of you are. That is my challenge for you. If you can get to it; the sword is yours." The Elf smirks in satisfaction.

"Consider it done. I'm going to put this little Elf in her place." Melanie seethes.

Before I can say anything, Melanie jumps into the water and sinks like a block of cement. The Elf stares after her in astonishment before grinning.

"She isn't even close, she will run out of air before she reaches it." The Elf girl laughs.

"Joke is on you. She doesn't have to breathe." Drew quips.

"What?" The Elf girl shrieks.

I watch Melanie, she turns her face and grins. Melanie then turns and walks towards the waterfall. I lose sight of her through the churning waters. Minutes tick by. The Elf shrieks again. I look in the water and see Melanie headed our way, with a large sword in her hand. Melanie breaks through the water, grinning wickedly at the Elf and holds the sword out to me.

"Oh how nice of you. You have retrieved the sword for me." A chilling, familiar voice calls out from across the top of the waterfall.

I look out to see over a dozen dark shapes forming at the top of the ridge, surrounding the waterfall fed pool.

CHAPTER 37

Melanie

"Tripp!" Avalon exclaims, astonished.

"That little bastard survived the flood?" I ask, not believing what I'm seeing

"Come and get it punks! You won't survive long. I promise you." Nickolai calls out.

A figure at the top of the hill gestures for the others around him to attack. Some fly, some jump down into the water and some run. Avalon, Braelomdrel, Zephyr and Rob take to the skies while Senna, Nickolai, Drew and I cover the ground.

"Well, this is new. Crap." I hear a voice mutter. I look around for its source and see one figure break off from the rest and run in the opposite direction of our group. I focus on the figure and see Tripp zoom into clear view.

"Tripp is on the run." I call out to the ones in the air.

"You guys dispatch these, I am going after him. He will go back with us to the Sidhe. We cannot allow him to return to Morcant!" Rob calls out to the group. Rob quickly angles downward, flapping his wings hard to pick up speed. He barely dodges past a few creatures in the air. Before they can strike him, Braelomdrel and Zephyr take out two, while Avalon hits another square in the chest with an icicle.

The cloudy sky opens up and it starts to rain. I grin, knowing what Avalon can do with this type of weather. These fools weren't counting on half of our group being able to fly. We got an upgrade since the last time we fought Morcant's people. I look to see Senna fighting off a couple with two wicked looking long swords. Where did she hide those?

I dispatch a Fae as it exits the water, it was only just forming ice weapons. I look over and find Drew and Nickolai. They look like animals playing with their prey. Each one facing down two as well, circling, jumping, weaving in and out clawing at their attackers.

"Quit playing and finish them off, there are plenty more!" I yell out.

Two more come out of the water and I can tell without looking too close that they are Vampires, both have their dagger-like nails extended, ready for a fight. They feel different than the ones back home. They seem older, stronger. Great. Instead of letting them have a chance to see and surround me, I attack the closest one first. Landing right in front of the first one, I thrust my hand out, burying it deep within her chest. She makes a surprised gurgling noise and collapses. My hand slides out of her body, clutching a still and bloody heart. I crush it to a big gooey mess.

Hands grasp my head and I can feel nails going into the sides of my neck. Shit! I try to reach for my attacker but fail. A third Vampire, I didn't see comes straight at me. I scream in rage while scared that my head is about to pop off at any freaking second. Suddenly the nails release and the hands fall from my body and I stagger. A grey blur shoots past me and I hear a loud thump, followed by sounds of flesh being torn. I look behind me to see Senna, with a smile on her blood covered face, holding the other Vampire's head by its hair. Quickly, I reach down and thrust my hand into the Vampire's body, bring out the heart, and crush it.

I take a moment to look around me and have that moment to yell at the others to brace themselves, as a large wave comes crashing down on us. As the water recedes, I look for the source and find Avalon looking down at me.

"Seriously, are you trying to kill us?" I yell.

"Sorry, I got a bit overzealous. Besides, those three can swim and survive a wave, and you can hold your breath for quite some time. I don't think anyone in our group was in danger of dying from that." Avalon says with a grin.

"True. We are too bad ass to be taken out like that." I counter, grinning back and take another look around.

The river and pools are over flowing with water. The ground around the pool is starting to flood.

"Please tell me you didn't flood a country this time?" I ask Avalon.

"Well, I hope not! I don't think so. This time does not feel anything like the last. I'm still here and coherent!" Avalon laughs nervously.

"It's about time you showed up. You missed all the fun. Unless you were able to have some fun on your own with that worthless piece of shit." Nickolai calls out to Rob, who had just landed with an unconscious Tripp in tow.

"Knocking Tripp out to take him to the Sidhe is not my idea of fun. We need to get information from him and I am hoping to rehabilitate him after." Rob states.

"Why would you waste your time, rehabilitating him?" Drew asks.

"He is not who you think. He was not born mortal and changed like you. Tripp chose to come to the mortal world, like Avalon's mother. Somewhere along the way, he met up with Morcant instead of our scouts." Rob says solemnly.

"Still I don't see why that should matter." Nickolai says.

"It matters because his name is not Tripp, it is Kieran. He is my brother." Rob says sadly.

CHAPTER 38

Braelomdrel

Faces of shock flood the group at the confession Rob lays on us, with the exception of Senna, Zephyr and myself. I have no clue who Tripp is or what he has done prior to this. Avalon never mentioned him before. No one in the Sidhe has mentioned the name Kieran within my hearing. A lost prince of the Seelie Court. You do not run into one of those every day.

"You have a place in mind on where to keep him then, when we get back home?" I ask.

"I do. There are some cells we hardly ever use for enemies of the Sidhe." Rob replies.

"I do not think you will be able to rehabilitate as planned by keeping him a prisoner in a cell. He must be gradually introduced to people he once knew. Relearn things he knew before going to the mortal world. Eventually, things may start to come back into his memory." Zephyr interjects.

"I do not want to dump him off with our parents." Rob scoffs.

"That would be the better thing to do honestly. You should not fear for the safety of your parents. They can handle themselves, and from what I remember of Kieran, he is not much of a threat to either of them." Zephyr points out.

Rob nods.

"So exactly how does everyone get back?" I ask.

"I've already booked flights for the three of us back home. We have to return the rental car anyway. I'll be reimbursed right? This just about wiped out my available funds on the credit card." Nickolai says and hands Avalon the sword.

"Yes. Once everyone is situated, I will get back in touch with you and get that taken care of." Rob advises.

"Avalon, can you manage to go back to the Sidhe and get Bain?" Zephyr inquires.

Avalon grins. "I think that can be managed. There is one thing I must do first before anything else."

Avalon moves the sword with both her hands and examines the pommel carefully, balancing the tip of the sword on the ground. A faint purple glow emanates from it. With deft fingers, she takes a small purple stone from the center of the pommel and brings it up to her necklace. The dragon within the pendant moves. It reaches out and takes the purple stone from her and brings it within the pendant.

I look around at those gathered and they seem to share my disbelief in what we just witnessed.

Avalon grins. Without saying a word, she takes a step towards us and vanishes. Within moments the large mass that is Bain stands before us.

"Where is Avalon?" I ask Bain.

"With King Finvarra, he was waiting with me for your return. Let us return in haste." Bain says quickly.

"Until we see each other again." I say and bid farewell to Drew, Nickolai and Melanie.

The fairy pools of Skye fade from view and the open courtyard of the palace surrounds us. King Finvarra looks to us in panic, holding Avalon awkwardly.

"Zephyr, I am so relieved you are here. She collapsed right after Bain left. She has a deep cut in her side." King Finvarra explains quickly.

Zephyr and I rush to Avalon's side. She moans slightly and goes silent. We slowly lower her to the ground. While Zephyr tends to her with medicines from his pouch I notice something is different. Her necklace is also missing. I look up and catch sight of a piece of metal the King is tucking into his sleeve.

"The King, he is hiding something. Her necklace is missing." I inform Rob quickly.

Rob hands Kieran over to Bain, and takes a hold of the

King, surprising him. From the sleeve drops the necklace. Seemingly from nowhere, a sword point is inches from the face of the King. Senna, with plugs in her ears, has the King under arrest.

"What are you doing? Are you daft girl?" Finvarra questions Senna.

"*Get him to a cell.*" I inform Senna.

"Unhand me! I am the King! Release me at once!" Finvarra bellows.

"I am not sure what the King has done, but my medicine is not working as it should. This is no wound she would have gotten at the pools." Zephyr says in worry.

"Search the area, call for extra hands to find whatever he used on her." I call out.

Within moments the courtyard fills with extra bodies all scouring the landscaping for anything amiss. Oonagh rushes over to where we are gathered, with worry etched on her face.

"Zephyr, what has happened? Will she be alright?" Oonagh asks.

"It appears the King injured her, with what we do not know, yet. I do not know if she will be alright either. I need to consult with Angeliss, she may be our only hope." Zephyr says solemnly, shaking his head.

"*Avalon.*" I try to reach her mind. I am met with utter silence.

Bain hands custody of Kieran over to Rob and then

disappears with Zephyr.

"Tend to your brother and then come back quickly. I will stay with Oonagh and we shall watch over Avalon." I tell Rob.

"You did not seem to look too surprised when Zephyr said the King was involved in this." I say quietly to Oonagh.

"Finvarra has been corrupt by power for centuries. I do not think he wanted anyone to ever succeed him." Oonagh said sadly. "There are several of us that have been waiting for something like this to happen."

I gape at her in shock.

"Do not misunderstand. I do not wish any harm to befall my grandchildren. However, his reaction to Rion when he arrived, and then Avalon, it seemed a matter of time. Now with his actions, he can be removed from power and the Heir will succeed him." Oonagh says and caresses Avalon's face.

"Oonagh, who is Angeliss?" I ask.

"Angeliss is an old friend. One I have not seen in ages, but she is willing to aid us when we are in great need. I believe Avalon qualifies." Oonagh says in confidence.

Zephyr reappears with Bain. Ever so gently, Bain picks up Avalon.

"Angeliss requests we bring Avalon to her now." Zephyr says.

"I will come with you." I advise him.

"No, no one is to come with me but Bain. I will not be allowed to stay while Angeliss does her work." Zephyr says quickly before vanishing with Bain and Avalon.

"What now?" I ask Oonagh.

"Now, you will help me and Rion prepare the path for Avalon when she is well. We must have all evidence ready against Finvarra. I will be calling upon the Dagda so that Finvarra can be deposed." Oonagh says, standing up and offering me a hand.

"How can you just go on so calmly?" I inquire.

"I have faith in my friend that she will do everything possible to heal Avalon. The rest must be done, even if Avalon should perish, as Rion is next in line. Finvarra cannot be allowed to continue." Oonagh informs me.

"Avalon, do not leave me. Get better. Fight whatever holds you!" I send my thoughts to her, hoping she can hear them.

CHAPTER 39

Avalon

"Welcome home!" Finvarra says with a smile.

"Bain, the others are waiting for you at the Fairy Pools in Glen Brittle." I say and send an image of the location to him.

Bain nods and disappears.

"I take it you were successful and have found the next piece?" Finvarra asks, looking about my body.

"We were." I smile showing him the sword.

"Ah. Good. Very good." Finvarra approaches with his arms spread out invitingly.

It's unsettling, but I know making a relationship with all members of my family is important. I move closer and join him in an embrace. I release him only to feel a sharp pain in my side. I look up at him in disbelief.

"None of my descendants will take the throne from me. You all plot against me. I will not stand for it!" Finvarra spits out with a sneer as he yanks the necklace off of me.

For a moment I stand there in confusion and shock. I have no idea what he is talking about. My vision clouds and starts to darken.

"What have you done to me?" I cry out in semi-blindness.

"Something you will never recover from my dear." Finvarra says with a sinister chuckle.

I try to respond but nothing comes out and my world is consumed by darkness. Voices drift in and out. I want to respond but can't. The pain spreads and the heat is almost unbearable. I feel Braelomdrel, his thoughts, but again I'm unable to respond. As swiftly as his thoughts come to me, they are gone and I'm left alone in the darkness.

~*~

Descendants! My mind is awake again. I don't know how long I've been out of it. I no longer feel hot but surprisingly cool, almost too much so. I can't move, see or speak. I try to mindspeak with whoever might be around me. Instead of a familiar mind, I'm greeted with more silence.

I think back upon what Finvarra said. Descendants. Who is plotting against him? I wasn't before, but I'm certainly against him now! The only other I can think of that wants the throne would be Morcant. A memory floods back, Finvarra and Morcant. Amberley said Finvarra has a brother. I stupidly assumed that was the answer. They aren't brothers. Finvarra is Morcant's father! The revelation only brings more questions. Who is his mother? Why is Morcant the way he is? Why is Morcant hell bent on controlling the Sidhe?

"Zephyr." A voice resonates around me, breaking me away from my internal musings. I do not recognize it, but it has a quality that seems familiar. "She will be waking soon. I was able to clear her body of the toxins. Make sure she rests after waking and drinks plenty of water."

"Our many thanks to you Angeliss. She is the future of our world." Zephyr replies with sincerity.

~*~

My eyelids finally decide to open after the umpteenth time of trying to move or see anything. A blurry colorful blob fills my vision like a psychedelic array. Amberley. I mentally sigh in relief.

"She is coming around! Go alert the Queen!" Amberley calls out and I wonder who she is talking to.

"I'll be right back!" Rion says swiftly and I hear the sound of his feet running across the room and the door shutting loudly.

"You gave us all quite the scare." Amberley says, her voice cracking. "Oonagh, Rion, Braelomdrel and Rob have all taken turns sitting with you."

"How long?" I manage to croak out.

"Zephyr brought you back to us two days ago. You have been gone for a week." Amberley replies, her eyes slightly wet.

I nod and lick my lips. My throat feels as if it is coated with sandpaper. Amberley hands a glass of water out for me. I try to move and take it from her, but my arm moves a mere three inches before it drops back onto the bed. Amberley puts the glass on my bedside table and sits near my head. She gently props me up and brings the glass to my lips so that I can drink. The water is cool and soothes my dry, itchy throat. I drain the glass and Amberley gently lays me back down.

The door to my suite opens again and I look toward the sitting room. Oonagh rushes in and breathes in a deep sigh of what appears to be relief. Rion follows close behind her with a smile on his face.

"I did not want to get my hopes up. To see you awake and alive brings me great joy and relief." Oonagh confesses.

I smile.

"I'm just glad you didn't leave me here to deal with all these crazies on my own." Rion says with a chuckle.

I laugh and grimace as a sharp pinch of pain radiates from my side.

"Does he know I still live?" I ask Oonagh.

Oonagh shakes her head. "He is still in a cell, alone. His only visitor has been an ear-plugged Senna to bring him food and drink."

"I would like to keep it that way." I croak out. I look over to the glass of water and pull out a small ball of water and bring it to my mouth. I drink it before continuing. "What happens next? Is there to be a trial?"

"The Dagda is here and has been waiting for you. He indicated there was information that you needed to be present for. The trial will be set for two days from now, to give you time to rest and recover." Oonagh informs me.

I nod, but wonder what the Dagda needs to tell me. I feel completely drained and close my eyes sinking farther back into the pillows. "I'm sorry but I need to sleep." I mutter out.

"Take the time you need to my dear. Anyone would need to after the ordeal you have gone through." Oonagh says and pats my hand gently.

I want to talk to her about Morcant and Finvarra but say nothing more. The look on her face told me she has gone through enough for now. In two days, it may all come to a head anyway. I hear Amberley usher Oonagh and Rion out of my room.

"*Amberley?*"

"*Yes, Princess?*"

"*I need to confide in you and obtain information. Can I trust that you will keep everything in confidence?*"

"*Of course, Princess!*"

"*Finvarra said that his descendants are plotting against him to take his throne after he stabbed me. When the Stone gave me a vision, I saw Finvarra clearly along with Morcant. I thought they might have been brothers after our talk. However, after Finvarra's admission, it seems*"

Morcant is his son. How is that possible?" An intense wave of shock passes through our link from Amberley.

"There were rumors that he had children before his marriage to your grandmother, but none ever surfaced. I know he was with Queen Mab for a time before your grandmother and she had a son, but that was a few years after your grandparents were wed. The boy was the spitting image of Mab last I saw him, but that was centuries ago."

"I need to arrange a meeting with Mab, Amberley. I have a strong suspicion that child is Morcant, and however he ended up on Earth is Finvarra's doing. Why else would he be so hell bent on taking control of the Sidhe. I think Finvarra attacked me because the people were taking a liking to me better than he expected."

"I will arrange for the meeting. It does seem plausible now that you mention this. He would see your growing popularity as a threat to his rule. Rion stated in public after you left that he had no intention of ruling the Sidhe unless there was no other choice. So the statement about descendants does not apply to him."

I say nothing more and drift off to the sounds of Amberley puttering about my room.

~*~

I sit still as Amberley sets my hair into intricate braids and curls. Just getting dressed is exhausting, but I'm happy that Amberley thought of this and adjusted my clothes and shoes so that they wouldn't be as cumbersome like before. Every day I have managed to do a bit more; such as walk around the room, eat, drink and complete other basic needs on my own. Zephyr came to see me last night to assess my progress for today's ordeal. He seemed pleased.

A knock sounds at the door just as Amberley puts the finishing touches in my hair. I turn in my chair to see who it is. Rion, Brae and Rob all walk in, dressed in their court clothes. No wonder Amberley put me into the same gown that I was introduced to the Council in.

"I thought we could all escort you. To assist if or when you feel weak and to disguise the fact should the need arise." Rob explains.

"Thank you. Is the gathering in the Great Hall?" I ask.

"It is. Are you ready?" Rob asks.

I nod and take his offered arm. We walk quietly towards the Great Hall, Rob on my left, Brae on the right and Rion behind me. We enter the great hall and the overly large man with red hair is the first person I notice. I remember him from Rob's story that night at my Dad's, the Dagda. The voices of the gathered masses is like a distant rolling thunder, just loud enough to be annoying.

Rob escorts me to the top of the dais. I thank him quietly and sit down next to my grandmother, leaving the High Throne empty. The Dagda looks at me and I nod my head. He nods in return and raises his hands, the gathered assembly silences.

"Bring forth Finvarra!" The Dagda's voice booms.

A side door opens and Senna escorts my grandfather into the room. A look of shock passes quickly over his face as he sees me sitting next to Oonagh, peering down at him, very much alive. I smile albeit grimly.

"My dear brother, how good it is to see you. Would you kindly tell them they were mistaken? I have done nothing wrong." Finvarra says with a sickeningly sweet voice, his eyes glittering a bright silver.

Brother? Holy crap! I look around and notice the looks change on the faces in the crowd, first the confusion and then defiance of what is going on. The feeling of foul oil creeps along my skin. I look to my grandmother, Rion, Rob and the others. They look back at me, each with a wink and quickly tap their ears. It is then that I notice; earplugs. I almost can't help laughing out loud, but manage to stifle it into a soft cough.

"You will use your true voice when talking to me!" The Dagda bellows.

My body breaks out in goosebumps. I've heard this before!

"I have been informed of your behavior over the past century, but it was the attack on Avalon that was the last straw. I know of the threat against the Sidhe and of your role in it." The Dagda says while glaring at a shocked Finvarra.

The assembly lets out an audible gasp following it up with whispers. I look at the Dagda. Does he know about Finvarra and Morcant?

"Yes, I know he fathered Morcant. As to what happened with Morcant and why he is coming after the Sidhe, I do not know."

The Dagda looks out at the assembly and the noise ceases.

"You are hereby stripped of all privilege, power and rank. You will be cast out into the world of man to thrive or die." The Dagda says with finality.

"People of the Sidhe, you will soon have a new High King and Queen. My son will be wed to Avalon and they will rule the Sidhe together until the end of days." The Dagda announces, turning to me.

Marriage? To who? Who is his son? No!

"I object!" Braelomdrel calls out.

The Dagda takes notice of Braelomdrel, seemingly for the first time and walks toward him. "You will have to go back to your mother. Your presence here will be a distraction and cannot be tolerated when my son arrives." The Dagda turns to me. "My son will be here for the wedding in two weeks' time. I will see you again soon, my dear."

A brilliant flash of light floods the room and when it dissipates, the Dagda and Braelomdrel are gone.

Seething and not waiting for anyone, I travel back to my room. I fall into the arms of a startled Amberley, completely drained. I shouldn't have done that. I'm so exhausted but too angry and disgusted to sleep.

"What is wrong? Did things not go well?" Amberley asks worriedly.

"Things went well, up until the time I was informed I would be marrying my cousin!" I scream in exasperation.

"What?" Amberley looks at me in shock.

"Yes, I just found out that the Dagda is Finvarra's brother! That makes him my Great Uncle or something, meaning any of his children are my cousins!" I rage.

"Which son?" Amberley asks.

"You can't be serious? I don't know which son. I didn't know he had more than one. I will not be marrying family and that is final. I don't give a rat's ass what he says. The only person to choose whom I will marry is me!"

Amberley looks taken back for a moment and grins.

"Well that is certainly good to know." Rob quips behind me.

I turn around and glare at him. "Ever heard of knocking?" I shriek.

"I did. You were too busy ranting." Rob says with a smirk.

"Oh. Well I'm tired of having my life dictated for me. Done with a capital D. No one is going to command my life but me!" I shout out, finally feeling my anger start to fizzle out.

"Then you are ready to be Queen in your own right. I cannot wait to see the look on his face when you tell the Dagda, my dear." An unfamiliar voice chimes in from behind me.

I turn around, thinking about how people do not knock here, to find Oonagh standing there next to a dark haired woman with amazing caramel and chocolate colored eyes.

Who is this stranger, and why does she seem so familiar?

GLOSSARY

For all those pesky words you might not know how to pronounce or what they are.

Sidhe – (Shee) The name for the Otherworld and the people that live there.

Merrow – The Irish term for Mermaid, Merman or Siren.

Tuatha De Danann – (Too-ah day Don-an) The supernatural race that settled in Ireland and fled to the Sidhe (Otherworld) and rule it to this day.

Samhain – (Sow-en) An Irish word for the holiday of Halloween.

Imbolc – (i –molg) An Irish word for the holiday marking the beginning of spring.

Oonagh – (ou –na) Avalon and Rion's Grandmother

ACKNOWLEDGMENTS

I give thanks to my husband, for taking care of our home and children. He took care of everything while I was out tending to the imaginary people in my head.

Thank you to my kids, for putting up with mommy's absence.

Melinda Fowler, my kickass proofreader, thanks for helping me polish up the mess of a first draft I gave you.

Thanks to my friends at the Hangout, for keeping me sane. Bouncing ideas off you guys has been a God send.

Did you enjoy this book? You can make a big difference!

Reviews are the most valuable tools authors have when it comes to getting attention for their books.

You can help out in a big way! If you enjoyed this book, I would appreciate it if you would take five minutes to leave a review.

Amazon:
https://www.amazon.com/dp/B01MU2F1CQ

Good Reads:
https://www.goodreads.com/book/show/33518045-altered

I invite you to follow me on Facebook, Twitter, Instagram and my website. These are the best places to reach me and I would love to chat about the characters and books with you. I look forward to hearing from you. You can follow along with me on updates and things across all of my accounts.

http://www.juliescholfield.com
http://facebook.com/JulieScholfieldBooks
http://twitter.com/JulieScholfield
http://instagram/julie.scholfield

ABOUT THE AUTHOR

Julie Scholfield was born in Stockton, California and fell in love with marine animals growing up near the Pacific Ocean. She currently lives in Northern Colorado. Julie loves to read fantasy novels, paint, and play with her kids.

Her first fantasy novel, Awakened was released on October 14th, 2014, the first of the series called Otherworld Origins. Altered, the second book in the series, was released on December 20, 2016. She is currently working on Ascended, the third book in the series.